The Silence of Echoes

The Secret of the Bird Cage Theatre

THE SILENCE OF ECHOES

THE SECRET OF THE BIRD CAGE THEATRE

MANUELA SCHNEIDER

WILL ROGERS MEDALLION WINNING AUTHOR

HAT CREEK

HAT CREEK

An Imprint of Roan & Weatherford Publishing Associates, LLC
Bentonville, Arkansas
www.roanweatherford.com

Library of Congress Cataloging-in-Publication Data
Names: Schneider, Manuela, author
Title: The Silence of Echoes: The Secret of the Bird Cage Theatre/Manuela Schneider
Description: Second Edition. | Bentonville: Hat Creek, 2024.
Identifiers: ISBN: 978-1-63373-905-5 (trade paperback) |
ISBN: 978-1-63373-906-2 (eBook)
Subjects: | BISAC: FICTION/Romance/Time Travell | FICTION/Romance/Paranormal |
FICTION/Mystery & Detective/Historial

Hat Creek trade paperback edition March, 2024

Cover Design by Casey W. Cowan
Interior Design and Electronic Formatting by Michele Jones
Editing by Amy Cowan

I dedicate this book to the soiled doves of Tombstone's red-light district and to the outstanding Bird Cage Theatre, one of the most iconic frontier saloons and brothels that ever existed. The shady ladies and their customers, including the hard-working miners, played an important role during the heydays of Tombstone.
Without either group of daring pioneers, Tombstone would never have grown into a big silver boom town and would have never lured the Earp Brothers or Doc Holliday into the town.

ACKNOWLEDGMENTS

Thanks to my wonderful editor Pam Van Allen who makes my books so much better and to the Hunley family to keep the wonderful Bird Cage Theatre alive to this day. The museum is a must see just like the entire town of Tombstone. Thanks to my family and friends for the support and to Roan & Weatherford for believing in me.

THE SILENCE OF ECHOES

THE SECRET OF THE BIRD CAGE THEATRE

CHAPTER 1

LATE EVENING SHIFT

*L*isa stepped out of the saloon's door onto the weathered boardwalk. The town was quiet and Allen Street deserted. The daytime tourists were gone and now either sleeping happily in their hotel rooms or had driven off to the next touristy town of interest.

She stuck a cigarette between her full lips and lit it with the Zippo lighter her boyfriend had given her for her last birthday. Lisa glanced at it as it reflected the light of the streetlamp in front of the business. Smiling, she returned the Zippo into her old, red purse.

Despite the chill, the tired woman remained standing in front of the saloon, smoking for a few minutes, inhaling the nicotine and trying to unwind from her shift as waitress. Then she flicked the cigarette away into the dusty street glancing at the flying sparks as they vanished.

She crossed her arms in front of her chest rubbing her hands over her upper arms and kept cursing the cold breeze. There was no way of getting warm in her short jacket.

"It is about time temperatures warm up. I will freeze one of these days," she mumbled, trying to cover her cleavage, which was emphasized with a dark green corsage. The outfits of the saloon girls were meant to attract guests but sure didn't function too well against cold nights in Arizona's high desert.

Turning right, she slowly walked along the boardwalk, and her boots produced a hollow sound with each step she took on the wooden planks. She gazed into the windows of the closed shops shaking her head at the usual bits and pieces arranged in them. "It would make sense to update those displays once in a while or at least dust the items," she tattled.

All the other bars and saloons had closed earlier than Big Nose Kate's, and not even a stray dog walked in the streets except for Lisa. She was on her way to her parked car at the parking lot below the small hill at the upper part of Allen Street.

It was a normal weekday, and even Kate's, as the locals called the saloon, had closed early due to the lack of paying guests. There hadn't been any live music today, and Lisa was bored with the same old songs being played on the house equipment on a constant repeat.

Big Nose Kate's was one of the best-known hangouts in the entire Southwest and drew visitors from all over the world who wanted to experience some Wild West flair. Unfortunately, the place hadn't been as busy as usual lately.

As a matter of fact, the entire town battled a dropping number of tourists these days. All shop owners complained constantly about lower sales during the past few months.

But instead of overthinking their marketing and the range of products offered on their premises, people blamed everyone else and the weak economy for the lousy balance results and the lack of business development.

To make things worse, Tombstone was similar to other places when it came to politics. It was small town affairs in every corner of the place, and changes, even for the better, were not welcomed easily.

This town depended on its visitors and their precious dollars. One thing was sure, the guests from all over the country had become stingy lately, not wanting to spend much cash in town, at least not like in the old days.

Folks fussed about having to pay admission to shows and museums, thinking the entire town was an open-air amusement park free of charge. Sadly, they mainly spent their money on food and drinks. The tourists seemed to forget that people in town had to pay their bills and come up with enough money to cover their cost of living.

Some stores closed only a few months after opening, not capable of surviving the low income.

A few days ago, Lisa and her co-workers discussed a newspaper interview in the *Sierra Vista Herald*. The town's mayor claimed that Tombstone drew over a million visitors each year, but Lisa and other townsfolk doubted that number. They were quite sure that he sugar-coated the truth.

"Well, can't change the situation today, so I'd better hit the road," she mumbled, feeling short of breath because she walked so fast trying to beat the cold on the way to her car.

Lisa's work colleagues knew well that she hated boring evening shifts with a small number of guests and avoided her mood swings whenever the saloon didn't have a crowd. What aggravated her even more were the lousy tips that resulted. Tonight, her shift had been never-ending, dragging for most members of the crew with the usual townsfolk around them.

She hadn't even paid attention to what the people had talked about at the bar. Everybody was a wannabe Wyatt Earp or Doc Holliday, and most claimed to be discovered in some movie to be produced soon by one of the countless indie movie producers. "Daydreamers," she scoffed.

The pretty waitress stopped in her tracks and searched for another cigarette as if smoking would help her to get warm. It was a bad habit, and she knew that she spent too much money on each packet of coffin nails as her boyfriend called them, not even mentioning the health issues smoking could cause.

She lit another one and left blood red marks from her lipstick on the butt. Small sparks glinted on the tip, and she searched for her car keys in her purse knowing that the lighting in the parking lot was rather poor.

She hadn't been aware that she stood right in front of the Bird Cage Theatre with its dark windows staring back at her like the eyes of a stranger. A sudden cold breeze touched her cheek, and she shivered. Lisa cautiously looked back at the facade of the building.

Her boyfriend constantly begged her to pay the theatre a visit with him. "They are said to have a lot of cool stuff in there, you know, like pioneer things. It was the most notorious honky tonk back in the days," he used to say trying to lure her into a walking tour through the former theatre and brothel.

But Lisa told him more than once that she had never liked the Bird Cage. In her opinion, it was the eeriest spot in town, and she had no intention of setting foot in that old building.

There was something about the place which didn't seem right to her. Lisa knew it was one of the few original structures from Tombstone's heydays that had survived the big fires of 1881 and 1882. Despite people being crazy over the museum it hosted, she was not willing to become a fan of the old shack.

Lisa wanted to get home as fast as possible and turned on her heel. She hurried past the dark building toward her car knowing that the goosebumps did not only cover her arms due to the cold breeze blowing. "Lord, I hate that old shed," she whispered.

She never shook off the chill even as she drove toward Sierra

Vista with the car's heater on full blast all the way to the parking lot of her apartment complex.

Four hours later on Allen Street, no one was out on the road at 1:45 a.m., not even a stray cat or one of the countless deer roaming through town.

The weather was calm, the night, dark with a slight trace of silvery moonlight peeking down on the streets from behind a few puffy clouds. Tombstone slept.

The former Bird Cage Theatre lay in complete darkness, but if anyone had been walking along the boardwalk, they would have heard the soft clinking of glasses as toasts were made, accompanied by the high-pitched giggles of fallen angels from days long gone.

Maybe someone would have even heard the muted sound of the old-fashioned piano drifting through the doors onto the empty street. But no one was outside at this late hour, and so the old building kept living its own life of a long-forgotten time undiscovered by the folks in their houses in the middle of the night.

CHAPTER 2

CITY GIRL OUT OF PLACE

*C*heryl was fuming with anger and cursed loudly. "Of all the places I applied to it has to be this god-forsaken Western town." She held the papers announcing her appointment with the Arizona State Parks organization in her hand and slammed down her coffee mug spilling some of the lukewarm beverage.

Studying tourism management included a trainee placement at a tourist site of interest.

At first, she had been delighted that Arizona State Parks had accepted her application. But the thrill vanished when she read that they signed her up for the Courthouse Museum in dusty Tombstone. Her hopes to work as a ranger in one of the major spots such as the Red Rock State Park or Lake Powell were shattered.

Cheryl had daydreamed about beach parties after work and water-skiing lessons, and now it looked like she would be placed in a small town in the middle of nowhere.

All she had ever heard about Tombstone was that the town reeked of Western history, and Hollywood had made some movies about that silver rush settlement and its gunslingers from a long-forgotten time. That was it, and she wasn't keen in getting to know more.

"Place of touristy interest. What a freaking joke. To hell with those *pistolero* wannabes and their stupid gunfight at the God knows what corral. I want to be at a location that easily draws thousands of people from all over the world a day."

Cheryl liked crowds. The busier a place, the better. After all, she was a real city girl. But according to the Arizona State Parks management, all other job openings were filled by the time they had decided to hire her, so Cheryl had no choice but to try to make the best of the situation.

"Oh well, it's only for four months, five at the most. The time will pass quickly," she mumbled and tried to reassure herself.

A few weeks later the young woman travelled from the fancy California district where she lived to Tucson by Southwest Airlines.

She was used to big buzzing airports like LAX and received her first cultural shock when she touched down in Tucson. The airport was about the size of a shoe box compared to Los Angeles, and the scale of it put her in a bad mood right away.

"Oh, mercy me, and this is supposed to be the second biggest city in the state?" she muttered under her breath while leaving the gate.

The arrival hall was not busy at all, and she walked briskly toward the luggage belts. The walls were decorated with Southwestern paintings and Native American patterns, but Cheryl had no eye for them. While she stood next to the luggage carousel, she frantically punched on the touchscreen of her brand-new iPhone and almost missed her red suitcase passing by. She pushed the phone into the back pocket of her designer denim and pulled her suitcase off the baggage claim cursing as she broke off the manicured fingernail on her left index finger.

She gazed along the moving carousel and waited for her second piece of luggage. Just because she had to fulfill a term of studies in "No Man's Land" didn't mean she'd have to look like a country bumpkin hillbilly, and so she brought more clothes than likely necessary.

Cheryl always tried her best to dress stylishly and would never have left the house without makeup or a decent hair style. She looked as if she stepped out of a fashion magazine most times.

Like countless women at the West coast, she had a taste for fashion and the newest products from the promising cosmetics industry. Dang sure required she kept quite a well-calculated budget each month. Living in California was costly enough. The attractive student didn't expect to meet Mister Perfect in a rustic Western town but had packed wisely, nevertheless. She preferred to always be prepared for every possible occasion. Why change old habits? So far, she had not found her Prince Charming but kept her eye out for him.

Cheryl was older than most of her fellow students. After a few years working as an advisor in the unsatisfying world of sales and marketing, she couldn't imagine doing that same job for the rest of her life, so she spontaneously resigned and decided on a career in tourism management. She hoped to be able to see unexplored areas of the United States or even different countries across the pond once she achieved her master's degree. It was high time for a new path in her life. Fortunately, she did not look as if she was in her mid-thirties already and hoped for a leading management position in a luxury resort in a year or two.

An older man in denims and a well-used cowboy hat walked toward her. "Excuse me, are you Cheryl Roberts?"

Cheryl turned, annoyed at first. Who addressed her so bluntly? But then she recalled an email in which the courthouse management had promised to send someone to pick her up. So, she showed her best smile and shook the man's hand.

"That's me! And you are...?"

"Bert McEntire, but call me Bert, please. We don't stand much on formalities in Tombstone."

"I bet you don't," Cheryl mumbled as she swung her travel bag around, almost hitting Bert's thigh.

Her second suitcase arrived, and she quickly pulled it off the baggage claim. Her luggage was quite a handful, but Bert was surprisingly trim and managed to pull the two bags without difficulty.

They left the arrival terminal, and he walked straight to the opposite parking lot. Cheryl blinked against the blazing afternoon sun. Bert threw the luggage into his white pickup and started the engine, which came alive with the rumbling sound of an angry cougar. After paying the parking fee at the booth, he drove past the airport motels and onto the interstate.

Cheryl hoped for a decent hotel room in Tombstone, but all she could imagine was a dusty miner's cabin with an outhouse. *Oh Lord, what an adventure*, she thought, already missing her comfortable apartment in Los Angeles. However, what she didn't miss at all was the crazy traffic of the city—six lanes that generally led nowhere, thanks to the daily traffic jams. It was pleasantly calm on the highway leading out of Tucson's suburbs. Compared to Los Angeles, the road toward Cochise County seemed deserted.

Who knows, we might even encounter an old stagecoach. She rolled her eyes at that thought.

From what Cheryl knew, thanks to Google Maps, the ride would take about an hour.

The farther they drove toward Tombstone, the more the scenery changed. It varied from bone-dry desert full of scrubs and thorns to a chain of hills visible on the horizon.

They took exit number twenty-six and entered the town of Benson, where Bert pulled into the parking lot of a Safeway store. He shut off the engine and laughed at Cheryl's puzzled look.

"I thought you might like to buy some groceries. You know, healthy food like cereals, soy milk, salads. Not much of a choice in Tombstone when it comes to grocery shopping, I have to admit. Well, at least we have a Dollar Store now and, of course, our Circle K gas station which isn't a real grocery store. But if you look for a Whole Foods or Trader Joe's which carry all the fancy Californian healthy food choices, then you are stranded in our little pioneer town."

He winked at her, and it was obvious that he was making fun of the California lifestyle of consuming healthy and fresh food. Bert locked the car, left her luggage on the back seat, and fetched a cart for her. She smiled at his gentlemanly manners.

Oh well, at least there's hope that I might come across some nice-acting people in the next few months. Maybe it won't only be rugged cowboys.

The Benson Safeway was surely far from the variety of Trader Joe's, and she already feared for her diet and figure, but at least she was able to buy the necessary stuff. It was actually quite thoughtful of the man to give her the chance to shop for food on the way. But after a few minutes as she pushed her cart toward the shelves filled with cereals, she turned to Bert and stopped dead in her tracks.

"Wait a minute, how am I going to keep all this in one motel room?" she asked, pointing at her cart which was filling up fast. "Do you happen to know if I have a small refrigerator in the room?"

He smiled. "Actually, you will have more than a small fridge in your temporary quarter. Since you'll be staying for a few months, the Park's management organized a small house for you. Cute place. It's an original Victorian from 1881. It belonged to one of the colorful madams from Tombstone's rowdy past."

She must have turned as pale as the eggshell-colored wall in the store because he quickly assured her that the amenities in the house were, of course, brought up to today's standards. However, Cheryl was not convinced at all and prepared herself for the worst. *Hopefully, I don't have to use an outhouse and water pump to shower or wash clothes,* she thought with a frown.

After paying and loading all the plastic bags behind the passenger seat, they drove onto Benson's main street and were on their way to their final destination.

Bert looked at her. "So, what do you know about Tombstone?"

Cheryl shrugged her shoulders. "Literally nothing," she admitted. "Wait, that's not true. I know that you had some famous gunfight in the 1880s, and Wyatt Earp was staying there and a man called Doc something...."

Bert laughed. "Doc Holliday, you mean. Yep, that pretty much sums up what most tourists know about Tombstone as well. You'll know much more about the place by the time you leave. I guarantee you that. There's something about Tombstone that sucks you into its history. And believe me, there's so much more of it there than that one famous gunfight. It's hard to explain. You have to experience it. One thing is sure, it is a special town and selects the people to whom she shows her true face and the adventures of her rowdy past. It seems rather like a village but is far more than just a collection of old buildings."

Cheryl stared at his profile. He spoke about the place as if it were a living person. *Oh Jesus, I'll probably end up with a bunch of cowboy-hat-wearing weirdos around me on a daily basis.* She wasn't really looking forward to the next few months. But what could she do? She needed the internship for her certificate or would fail the entire course, and she had invested too much money into her studies already.

When they got closer to Tombstone's town limits, Cheryl saw a rugged canyon to the left and asked Bert what the area was called.

"That's Cochise's Stronghold. It's part of the Dragoon Mountains and used to be the hiding spot of the famous Geronimo and Cochise and their renegade band of Chiricahua Apache. You'd be surprised at the interesting historical places you can find all around Cochise County."

Cheryl had her doubts about that, as she wasn't into frontier history, but didn't want to offend Bert. After all, he'd been very nice to her.

The road they drove on had a few ditches, and numerous hills hid the town until travelers drew quite near. Merely five miles before the city limits, she finally saw Tombstone sitting atop one of the hills. To Cheryl's surprise, there was a checkpoint staged by the local Border Patrol on the left side of the road, and Bert slowed down.

"Wow, are they protecting the town?"

Bert shook his head. "We have many illegal immigrants crossing the border between here and Old Mexico. The Border Patrol fellows try to catch as many as possible and take them back across the border once they've registered the illegals' fingerprints. It's a sad sight and surely doesn't help our tourism at all. The bad part is, many smuggle drugs, and that has quite a tragic impact on society around this area. Some of the drug dealers are mighty dangerous. The number of guys they catch is a drop of water on a hot rock."

The pretty student studied the guys in uniforms and their threatening-looking dogs waiting patiently in the backs of the patrol cars.

Welcome to the Wild West, she told herself. Cheryl stared at the guns and handcuffs attached to the officers' belts. But the sight was known to her. In California, they had their own share of undocumented migrants and the problems associated with that topic. They drove past the checkpoint, and Bert waved at the officers who obviously knew him.

On top of the last hill, the first buildings of their destination welcomed them. To the right they passed two hotels and an RV park, and to the left she saw a sign that read "Boot Hill."

"So, you built your cemetery right at the entrance of town? What a welcome for visitors," she added sarcastically.

Bert looked over at her. "The cemetery is actually a real tourist attraction, as that's where some of the most impressive characters of Tombstone's past are buried."

"Well, as far as I know, neither the Earp brothers nor the notorious Doc Holliday are laid to rest there."

Bert remained silent for a moment. "True, they're not, but their victims surely are. As a matter of fact, Tombstone has two cemeteries."

"You're kidding me. Such a small town has two burial grounds? That seems as if people mainly came here to die in the old days!" It had slipped out of Cheryl's mouth before she realized how rude it may sound. *What do you know, girl? Maybe he has family members buried there. You better watch your mouth before you annoy folks right from the start,* she thought and blushed.

Bert didn't answer right away, and she was afraid he was offended.

But then he looked at her and said, "Many died here in the old days and a lot still do. The cause is a similar one. Those days, chances were high to run into a lead bullet, and these days, folks often end up with cancer due to the numerous lead water pipes still being used." With a stern expression, he added "And some folks never leave."

Cheryl found that an utterly strange thing to say, and goose bumps appeared on her arms. She had no clue what he meant and wasn't about to ask either, for fear of appearing disrespectful.

They drove along Fremont Street and then took a right turn to the Courthouse Museum. It was a lovely Victorian-style brick building, one of the tallest in town. Cheryl loved the white stucco window frames right from the start. Surprisingly, Bert didn't stop at the building but drove a bit farther down the road, stopping in front of a small, cozy-looking Victorian house. It had a nice, small garden, and a white picket fence lined the perimeter. The house was painted white, and its blue-grayish shutters added to the buildings cute appearance. The front door displayed colorful stained glass with a hummingbird design, and there was a simple rocking chair on the front porch. An archway covered by a lush rose bush in full bloom framed the entrance to the garden. The house was within walking distance of the courthouse, and the road was quiet, not crowded with cars or people. Cheryl loved her temporary domicile the moment she saw it and was anxious to go inside. It almost looked like a doll house, well restored.

As she helped Bert carry some of her luggage onto the porch, the sudden explosion of gunfire made her jump. But he only laughed.

"Don't worry! That was a reenactor of one of the gun shows scaring some tourists. Shooting blanks—no real bullets used, at least most of the time," he added with a boyish grin.

Cheryl nodded. She remembered a Tombstone story in the news about a shooting accident during a celebration of some sort about three years ago. She didn't know if she should be relieved or even more concerned about her stay in this town. It looked like she had arrived right in the middle of some modern version of the *Gun Smoke* television series.

Bert opened the house, handed over the keys, and carried her groceries and luggage into the living room and kitchen. Finally, he shook her hand.

"We'll see you tomorrow morning at the museum, then. Come to the front entrance at 9:00 a.m. Enjoy your first night in Tombstone and get some rest. You must be tired from traveling. Here's my card in case you need anything. My cell phone number is written on the back. Feel free to contact me any time."

"Thank you so much for your kindness, Bert. I'll see you tomorrow." He waved, jumped into his pickup truck, and drove off.

CHAPTER 3

ARRIVING IN TOMBSTONE

*C*heryl walked through what would be her temporary home for the next few months to come. It was small, all right, but it was definitely much better than having a tiny one-room hotel accommodation. At least she had enough space to put away all her clothes and prepare herself a meal. The front door led right into the living room. A tiny country kitchen offered a view into the front garden, and a cozy bedroom lay at the back of the house away from eventual street noise. The bathroom was small but very cute, with an old-fashioned, claw-footed bathtub, which also offered the possibility of taking a shower behind a lace-covered shower curtain.

The interior of the house was decorated with antique furniture. A lot of pictures on the walls showed scenes from the once-so-glorious past of Tombstone.

I wonder what it was like living here in those days, she mused. Although she was very much into modern architecture, she somehow liked the charming place right from the minute she set foot in it. Strangely, the furniture seemed almost familiar to her, and she loved the creaking hardwood floor.

To her greatest relief, she realized that she could dig this place for the next few months. However, whether she could get used to the Western town itself was a completely different story. Her doubts about that remained. But since the accommodation felt comfortable, she began to open up to the fact that she would spend the next four-to-five months here. The eager student was actually looking forward to her first day at work now. Cheryl was the kind of person who always made the best out of each situation life presented her with, and she intended to do the same here in Tombstone.

The attractive woman put away her groceries in the kitchen and started the coffee machine right away. What would she do without a strong brew? Her friends in California always made fun of her, calling her a coffee junkie. Most likely they were right about that considering the number of cups she drank every day.

She hauled the heavy luggage into the small bedroom and started unpacking her clothes.

Meanwhile, the delicious aroma of the brewing coffee wafted through the entire house like an exquisite perfume. It was quite a challenge for her to put all her belongings into the closet and chest of drawers without creating a picture of absolute chaos in the bedroom.

Once she was done, the place almost looked like a real home. She poured herself a big mug of coffee and sat in the rocking chair outside on the porch, savoring the taste of the hot beverage while she admired the rose bush with its white flowers. She caught a whiff of the blooming roses in combination with the coffee's rich aroma coming from her mug and started to unwind from the tough day.

So, this is Tombstone. She glanced up and down the street. It was a quiet town. No cars drove along this side street at the moment, and the actors of the gun shows were done for the day. The temperature cooled down, and she watched the magnificent colors of the sunset. The sudden chill Cheryl felt surprised her despite the previous heat of the day.

But then she remembered Tombstone's high elevation and went inside, grabbed a shawl to wrap around her shoulders, and refilled her cup. She returned to the porch and enjoyed the evening. Sudden movement caught her eye and almost caused her to spill the hot liquid. She couldn't believe it.

A deer stood only a few feet away, watching her which its huge brown eyes. "Hello, John Deer," she called out and laughed at her own joke.

Cheryl yawned and decided to call it a day. Exploring the town would have to wait until later this week. She was tired from traveling and went inside for a shower. After all, a new job waited for her the next day even if it was only a temporary one.

Before she crawled under the bed covers, Cheryl turned off the air conditioning. It was a simple unit, but it worked well and kept the small house cool during the day. She didn't need the AC in the evening as the temperature dropped more than it did back home in L.A.

The difference was that the air was not just drier here but also much less polluted compared to Los Angeles.

She snuggled deeper into the cozy blanket that lay across the old-fashioned iron bed and looked around the room. Its appearance resembled the perfect image of a Victorian era magazine. Strung crystals dangled from the shade of the lamp on the nightstand, causing hundreds of shiny little stars to reflect onto the old-fashioned floral wallpaper. The place was absolutely lovely. You could almost call it romantic. And with that thought, Cheryl turned off the light and drifted into a deep slumber.

LATE AT NIGHT, a lonely coyote howled on one of the hills, calling for his mate. It was far past midnight. The main museum room of the Bird Cage Theatre lay in darkness. Only the emergency exit lights produced a weak, neon green gleam around the stairs leading through the different sections of the theatre.

The light seemed out of place and added to the ghostly atmosphere in the room with its shadowy corners. The worn piano stood silent in front of the big stage with its old, dusty, faded curtains, waiting for someone to play it. The building was cool inside, thanks to the adobe walls.

To protect the countless artifacts of Tombstone's glorious past, it was strictly prohibited to smoke in the building. Everything inside the different rooms was dry as bones in the desert except for the bottles of old beverages that stood on the shelf of the antique bar near the entrance of the famous establishment. The darkness and the additional plywood wall added in later years made it impossible for anyone to peer through the windows into the theatre room behind the entrance, hence nobody saw the thick cigar smoke swirling toward the ceiling in front of the stage as if dozens of men enjoyed the aroma of tobacco while watching a performance.

Thanks to the dimness in the bar area, nobody witnessed how the beverages in the bottles kept on the counter for decoration gently swayed from side to side as if drinks had just been poured. The Bird Cage was alive.

CHAPTER 4

THE COURTHOUSE

*T*he next morning Cheryl woke early and stretched, lingering under the warm covers a few more moments. She had had some weird dreams about long calico dresses and old saloon music, but nevertheless, felt relaxed. It was time for coffee and some oatmeal, and off she would be to her first day at the Courthouse Museum.

Cheryl dressed in her favorite denims and a fancy blouse, brushed her hair, and added light daytime makeup which emphasized her dark green eyes. Then she walked over to the museum, arriving ten minutes early just as Bert McEntire turned around the corner.

"Howdy, Miss Roberts." He greeted her in a friendly manner and tipped his cowboy hat.

"Call me Cheryl if you don't mind. After all, we will see each other every day. No need to be formal, I would say."

"Okay, Cheryl, then. I hope you slept well?"

"Yes, I did. I love that little house. It's so cozy, and all the antiques add to its charm in a special way."

Bert nodded, then he pointed toward the parking lot. "Here comes my wife, Dorothea."

A woman in her late fifties walked toward them and started to talk with quite a raspy voice. "Good morning, Cheryl Roberts. What a pleasure to have you with us."

"Thank   you,   ma'am.   The   pleasure   is   all   mine, Missus McEntire."

The elder woman smiled warmly. "Call me Dorothea. So, you say you like your little temporary home? I'm glad you enjoy the interior of the place. Actually, some of the furniture belonged to my great-grandmother who ran one of the houses of ill repute here in town. She was French."

Cheryl liked Bert's wife immediately. Her face was weathered from working in the sun, her handshake was firm, and her smile warm and welcoming.

"Let me show you around, and then I'll explain what your job for today will be until you know the museum a bit better." Cheryl picked up her purse and dutifully followed Dorothea McEntire.

"You can leave your bag in the room behind our cashier booth. Nobody has access there but us. First, I'll give you a quick tour through the museum. It is important for you to know the different rooms and get an overview of the exhibition. Of course, you can have a closer look at the objects in the late afternoon. I suggest you stay with me in the booth today so you can handle the admission fee the visitors have to pay. Not much to learn for that. Pretty easy to operate our credit card terminal. But first, let's take a quick round through our lovely courthouse."

Dorothea smiled and winked at Cheryl who followed, smiling back at her. The first chamber to the right showed smaller artifacts in glass displays. According to the signs, some of them had even belonged to the famous Wyatt Earp, like his engraved silver pocket watch and a personal straight razor.

Cheryl would have to check them out later when she had more time, maybe after they closed for the day.

Dorothea and her trainee walked from room to room. The museum had many items displayed from Tombstone's colorful past. There were a lot of mining tools and equipment, horse buggies, weapons, even an original courtroom arranged with all its antique furniture and bookshelves full of old law books and town documents. The younger woman wondered what kind of trials had been held here in the old days.

Household items, ranching equipment, a safe—you name it, and it was there, displayed nicely in different showcases or on pedestals. The courthouse was more or less like a color picture book of Tombstone's heyday. To her surprise, Cheryl was looking forward to exploring all of the artifacts during the next few weeks. She had never been into Wild West history, but somehow this small museum drew her to learn more about it. After all, she had to write a long and detailed essay about her training experience here. It would be ideal to find a specific topic to write about. She was astonished she felt interested in the history now, merely twenty-four hours after arrival in a town she hadn't even wanted to be in to begin with.

Cheryl decided to make the best out of the situation and to learn as much as possible for her studies. After all, she was an ambitious type of student.

Dorothea explained the cashier equipment and which fees to charge for the different people. She was a humble and patient teacher, and it didn't take long for Cheryl to manage the cash register alone while Dorothea handled a group of visitors, guiding them through the place.

Around lunch time, Bert came by with a basket of fresh sandwiches, cold bottles of Mountain Dew soda, and Dorothea had the coffee maker running. To her surprise, they shared their lunch with Cheryl.

One thing is sure, they are really nice people and not so selfish like most city people tend to be, Cheryl mused while chewing on a delicious turkey sandwich. What surprised her even more was the rich taste of the coffee Bert offered.

He laughed. "It's Arbuckle, my dear, real cowboy coffee with a long history."

Cheryl nodded. "I dang sure could get used to this brew."

The three laughed. After half an hour they went back to work, and the afternoon went by quickly. The place wasn't busy on this weekday, and Dorothea encouraged Cheryl to take a stroll alone through the entire museum in the late afternoon.

The student walked from room to room and admired the old furniture and items displayed. She was astonished at how many chemicals had been used for silver processing in the old days and shook her head at the countless bottles of mercury. "Wow, I wonder if they knew how dangerous that stuff is?" she mumbled. She walked by a showcase full of medical equipment that had belonged to one Doctor Goodfellow. *What a suitable name for a doctor,* Cheryl thought and chuckled. But after reading the information about the good doc, she was mighty impressed. It seemed that he had been a doctor with very advanced knowledge, considering the medical standards in those days. He even did surgeries right here in this small town.

Holy cow, I don't even want to imagine having to undergo a gunshot wound surgery without today's medical procedures. The thought left her shivering.

She followed the signs leading her from one room to the next and eventually upstairs to the second floor. She was awestruck as she climbed the beautifully crafted wooden stairway. The stairs were worn and scratched but still gorgeous to look at, and the banister felt so smooth under her touch. After strolling through every upstairs chamber, Cheryl couldn't help but admire how amazingly the museum was equipped. Obviously, people had put in a lot of passion and love for the town's history.

The sun was already setting when Cheryl walked toward the side entrance close to the courtroom that led into the backyard of the museum. To her surprise, she saw ropes dangling from the gallows. She shuddered in spite of the last warm rays of the setting sun.

So even hangings took place here? Maybe it's just a decoration. I'll ask Bert about it.

As she turned to find Bert standing right behind her, she jumped. He slowly nodded and answered her unspoken question right away as if he could read her mind.

"Yes, Cheryl, seven men were hanged in this courtyard over the years. Tombstone was the county seat of Cochise for quite a few years, therefore, trials and executions were held right here. Saved folks the long ride to Tucson. Sometimes, you might still witness a man dangling on one of those ropes."

Cheryl thought the man was pulling her leg, but looking at his face, she saw he was dead serious. *No pun intended.* She didn't dare laugh.

Walking back into the museum, she noticed the sunset behind the courthouse was a beautiful sight but didn't look back over her shoulder. The fact that the gallows were not just some decorations for tourist selfies made her nervous.

In the evening, the California student walked along famous Allen Street, the center of Tombstone's tourist attractions. She decided to celebrate her arrival in the "Wild West" with a juicy steak at the Longhorn Restaurant which Bert had highly recommended.

It was interesting to walk along the boardwalk and glance into the windows of the tourist shops. The two major saloons, Crystal Palace and Big Nose Kate's, weren't busy, but it was still early. *People probably don't go out much on Thursday evening,* she guessed.

Her dinner at the Longhorn was delicious. Cheryl read the older server's name tag. *Donna.* The woman welcomed her in a casual way as if the two knew each other for years. In Los Angeles, Cheryl was well used to the anonymous treatment, but in this Western restaurant, she enjoyed the humble friendliness.

The sizzling steak, baked potato, and homemade coleslaw were mouthwatering. Cheryl was so full, and when she was counting the dollar bills onto the table, she said, "Donna, that was so delicious, but now I am stuffed like a Thanksgiving turkey, and you might need to roll me down the street. I am afraid I cannot move anymore." Both women laughed, and Donna waved at her as she left the restaurant.

The California student walked back to her little Victorian accommodation enjoying moving around in the cool evening air after the filling dinner. Music drifted out of Big Nose Kate's saloon, but she walked by it without peeking into the door.

When Cheryl arrived at her temporary home she decided to hang out on the porch for a little while. She watched two deer trotting along the road toward the RV Park, probably on the hunt for food. Looking to the sky, Cheryl realized she had never seen so many stars in the night as here in Tombstone. The Milky Way showed perfectly in all its beauty. One hardly ever saw stars in L.A. due to hundreds of thousands of streetlights.

Also, the quiet was a new experience for her. Cheryl would never have believed it if someone had told her so before, but to her surprise she enjoyed the silence and the darkness enveloping her.

She studied the night sky and was suddenly surprised to hear a soft whisper. "Mae!" Cheryl looked around, but no one could be seen.

Maybe sounds from down the street playing tricks on my mind.

Relaxing again, she moved the rocking chair back and forth to a rhythmic but creaky sound. The voice sounded again. "Mae, come to me, my love!"

Cheryl earnestly searched the darkness. Still, no one was visible in front of the house. She shook her head and went inside. *My ears make up things because this city girl is just not used to the quiet of the desert. Or maybe it was that big dinner lulling me into dreamland. Time to hit the sack anyway.* She got up and walked inside the house, closed the door behind her, and switched off the porch light.

CHAPTER 5

MAKING FRIENDS

*D*elicate rays of moonlight covered the sleeping town like a veil of silvery lace. At half past two in the morning, the theatre sat on the end of the street, waiting for its guests as it always had since it first opened in the winter of 1881.

A soft whisper murmured from a booth next to the stage. "She's back just as she promised so many decades ago. Mae has returned. I won't let her go this time. She belongs to me. She belongs to Tombstone."

The deep, pleasant voice faded into the darkness, accompanied by the aroma of cherry cigars. "I am not in a hurry for her to return and have waited over one hundred thirty years within these old walls. For me it seems like days because I have eternity on my side," the voice whispered. "She will find her way back to me, I know. She found me over a century ago, and she will be back in my arms soon."

Cheryl slept, but frightening dreams of gallows with ropes swaying in a gentle breeze haunted her. The next morning, she yawned and felt tired despite her eight hours of sleep. With a second cup of strong coffee, she tried her best to hide how dragged out she felt upon arriving at the museum. Cheryl didn't want to appear moody with her new bosses or the tourist visitors.

The following days went by so fast. The Courthouse Museum was busier on the weekends, and Cheryl's evenings were occupied with taking notes for the essay and studying her tourism management books. There was a lot of noise coming from the saloons on Friday and Saturday nights, and the young woman avoided them since they were mostly packed with drunken men. Some females painted their noses, too—at least the ones who wanted to show off or act tough. They behaved too loud and rather rowdy, far from ladylike.

Cheryl wasn't into drinking and knew how alcohol can change people's behavior, most times not for the better. She preferred not to make a fool of herself in public and stuck to her healthy lifestyle without cigarettes or booze.

On Monday, Dorothea invited Cheryl to accompany her to buy some groceries in the city of Sierra Vista about twenty miles from Tombstone, and Cheryl gladly accepted. It was nice to get out of town for a little while, and stocking up on groceries was a good idea since she couldn't afford to eat at restaurants every day. It would shrink her budget much too quickly. Dorothea showed her everything available in Sierra Vista, even a hairdresser, which would surely come in handy in a few weeks. The student enjoyed the other woman's company a great deal. The older lady seemed to be more sophisticated than Cheryl had first expected.

"Have you always lived in Tombstone, Dorothea?" Cheryl hoped she wasn't being too nosy but wondered how one could live a whole lifetime in a small town. Dorothea shook her head.

"You may not believe it, but we used to live right in the center of San Diego."

The girl coming from California herself was quite surprised

to hear that and raised her eyebrows. "What in the world made you move to a small settlement like Tombstone?"

"Well, the first time we sat foot into town was during a vacation trip with our RV over twenty years ago. We had toured pretty much all of Arizona and Utah. The Grand Canyon, Bryce Canyon, Arches National Park—we've seen it all. On the way back to San Diego we decided to take the southern route and stopped here for the night. We got hooked right from the first minute we arrived. The history is fascinating. It's difficult to explain, but there is something about Tombstone that doesn't let go of you. It's like stepping back in time. We returned often after that first stay, and when Bert retired from his engineering job, we finally decided to move here.

"Good part is, it's much cheaper to live here than in San Diego. Then, two years after we settled here, the position as director of the museum became available, and we decided to go for it. But once a year we still take a vacation with our RV.

"I have to admit that California has become way too hectic and crowded for us. We'll never be tempted to return there to live. We'd rather go to Utah or New Mexico, even Colorado. No, my dear, I don't miss California at all, well maybe except for the beach and the ocean."

I could never imagine living in a town the size of a small village. I need Californian culture, sports facilities, day spas, shopping centers, Hollywood, and all the fancy restaurants, Cheryl thought. *I'd probably die of boredom if I had to live in a place like Tombstone for good. Not to mention all the gossip that follows people's every move in such a tiny community.*

"I know that crime is bad, especially in Los Angeles, and the traffic and the pollution is disgusting. You are also right about the exorbitant cost of living there. But you can't have all the amenities without the negative stuff. There's always good with the bad, right? I definitely love the lifestyle of a big city."

Dorothea nodded as the waitress served their lunch. "Everybody has to select what suits us best. You might change your opinion when you get older. You know, when Bert and I were young we would have never considered leaving San Diego."

The two women enjoyed a salad together, some iced tea, and went shopping for groceries after finishing their meal. Cheryl was surprised at the many choices of European food in the store, and Dorothea explained that the variety was available thanks to the Fort Huachuca military base. Apparently, the army guys brought their taste for different specialties from all over the world. And sometimes they even brought a wife from overseas. No wonder one could find Polish sausages, German dark bread, or even smoked Black Forest ham in the local grocery stores.

They loaded everything into Bert's pickup, and on the drive back to Tombstone they chatted about the house where Cheryl was staying.

"I really love it. It's super comfortable, and although small, it's really cozy."

Dorothea nodded. "It was the living quarters of a real madam of Tombstone's red-light district. She was one of my ancestors." Cheryl blushed, but Dorothea laughed.

"I found out about having a connection to Tombstone's past once Bert and I roamed through a heap of city papers. You can imagine my surprise. Maybe that is the reason why I felt drawn to this town right from the start."

"Must have been quite a shock for you," Cheryl said. "I mean, a madam and prostitute as an ancestor is not really what one would expect in the family tree, right?"

Dorothea shrugged her shoulders. "There's nothing to feel ashamed about. Those days, women didn't have much of a choice to earn their own money. There was a big demand for ladies of the line in Tombstone, actually across the whole frontier. Females were highly outnumbered. Therefore, the miners and gamblers, gunfighters, and cowboys would pay any price for a lady's affection, even if she were no lady at all. To a certain extent, you might say that men knew the value of a woman better in those days than they do now. No wonder many women went for that source of steady income. Some had a choice, but most had none."

Cheryl had never thought of it from that point of view, and she had to agree with Dorothea.

"In case you're worried, I can reassure you that Crazy Anne never performed her trade in the house where you are staying. Rather, she managed one of the brothels in town. Well-known as a 'calico queen,' she mainly performed at the Bird Cage Theatre up on Allen Street."

"Performed?"

Dorothea smiled.

"Yes, she ran a group of can-can dancers, and they did quite daring choreographies in very revealing costumes, if you want to believe the historical papers."

Cheryl was amazed at the woman's extensive knowledge of the town's past and its red-light district and told her so.

"You know, sometimes this town doesn't offer you much of a choice. It confronts you with its colorful history sooner or later when you least expect it. Tombstone has a way of communicating with some people in quite outstanding, sometimes tragic ways."

Cheryl had no clue what she meant and waited for further explanation, but it didn't come. Dorothea dropped the subject as fast as it had come up.

The rest of the day went by quickly, and, to her taste, too soon Cheryl found herself standing in front of her guest house again when Dorothea dropped her off. Groceries in hand, she waved goodnight to her new friend.

It had been a nice day. She stacked away the food she had

bought and was looking forward to the increased variety for dinner in her fridge. She brewed a cup of her beloved coffee and sat outside on her rocking chair, which was fast becoming her favorite spot of the house.

The sun set in gorgeous crimson and orange colors, and a lonely coyote yipped from between the hills far behind the garden. Cheryl felt content, although she remembered grumbling in the beginning about being assigned to Tombstone. Now she loved this homely little place where she lived for the time being. Yes, it somehow strangely felt like home.

CHAPTER 6

DISAPPEARING

*L*isa left the saloon later than usual, and despite her normal routine to avoid the direct route from Big Nose Kate's to her parking space at the bottom of the hill behind the Bird Cage Theatre, she walked right by the back side of the dark building this time.

"Screw this dang old brothel. I just want to get home," she mumbled under her breath.

Dead tired, her feet were throbbing. She worked a double shift because one of the bartenders had called in sick with the flu barely an hour before his shift started, so Lisa had to stay behind another five endless hours. She was angry with her boss for demanding that from her and told him so, but when he suggested that she could stay at home if she didn't like the job any longer, she backed down as she needed the income and did not dare refuse taking on the extra time. At least Lisa made a good number of tips today. The bad part was that her fiancé was most likely upset with her now since she had to call off their date for a movie over in Sierra Vista.

Passing the outer wall of the building's back at a brisk stride, she heard a moaning sound. It was something that often occurred in old adobe structures because of the late-night temperature drop. It didn't worry her much. When the small parking lot came into sight, it was too dark to make out her car. "It's about time that darn city council comes up with the additional streetlights they promised," she cussed.

"Dang, if it was for the tourists, the silly lights would shine all over the place like a freaking Christmas tree by now," Lisa mumbled under her breath, apparently upset about having to search her way with the dim light of her cell phone.

"A silver dollar should be enough for you, little bird."

Lisa spun around, nearly losing her balance on those stupid stilettos while she tried to figure out where the voice had come from. She wasn't in the mood for a bad joke pulled by some drunken coward hiding behind a corner. She glanced back at Allen Street, but no one was there. So, she shook her head and was just about to continue her walk toward the car when she heard the voice again.

"Come on over. I said, I'll pay you well!"

Lisa looked nervously over her shoulder again, obviously worried now. Cold sweat covered her forehead.

"Who are you? I've got mace, and I'm calling nine-one-one if you don't leave me alone."

No answer. The waitress turned around, ready to run. As she passed the rear wall of the former brothel, an old wooden door opened with a shrieking sound from its rusty hinges. In all the years Lisa had been working at Big Nose Kate's, she had never realized there was another door into the historic building. But before she could consider it, she was yanked back brutally by a steely grip on her neck and pulled into the building. She wanted to fight the dark shadow of a man she had never seen before, frantically trying to get away. But she didn't have a chance. The door closed behind her with a loud noise. Her screams in the depths of the museum's basement remained unheard above in the streets of Tombstone. Nobody saw what happened. No soul came to help her.

The next morning tourists and locals drove down the hill behind the town's center and parked next to Lisa's little red car. The day promised to be a bustling one.

As people walked by the building known as a historic brothel and saloon, they didn't pay any attention to the rear wall. It was only an adobe wall, old with its fading, brownish color chipping off. Nothing to see there except for some bushy grass. The main entrance to the Bird Cage faced Allen Street, and the backside of it offered neither an entrance nor an exit for its visitors.

The owner of Big Nose Kate's saloon was angry with his employees and slammed his big hand onto the bar counter while he tried Lisa's phone, but nobody answered.

He turned to his friend sitting at the bar. "At least John, had the guts to call in sick. Lisa is probably so mad at me for having to work his shift after her own that she won't even call to let me know where the heck she is. Simply doesn't show up for work. Can you believe that? Man, I tell you, it gets harder and harder to find decent employees."

His friend sipped his fresh coffee and nodded in agreement. He ran the shop opposite the saloon and had seen his share of unreliable employees over the years. Every morning he would pay a visit to the saloon for an additional cup of coffee. He gulped the rest of his beverage, and both men wished each other a successful morning. While the saloon owner watched him walk across the street to open his souvenir shop, he still cussed and grumbled about Lisa not showing up for work.

No one heard anything from her over the next forty-eight

hours while her little red car sat lonely and shimmering in the day's heat in the parking lot.

Nobody caught the shiny reflection of her car keys in the stubby, dry grass at the wall of the backside of the old structure.

CHAPTER 7

EVENING STROLL

*C*heryl had been in town for more than three weeks. She had learned about the famous gunfight at the O.K. Corral between the Earp brothers, Doc Holliday, and a gang of cowboys. By now she also knew some facts about the notorious Doc Holliday and somehow couldn't help but wonder what the men involved in that deadly conflict so many decades ago would say if they knew how their killing reputation was still being celebrated nowadays. A lot of people even saw them as national heroes. Question was if those men would be proud of their doings as well.

In Cheryl's eyes it was not a heroic story. In her opinion, the gunfight was merely the logical consequence of a long-term, smoldering conflict back in a time when men wore weapons and used them to end an argument.

She shook her head in disbelief when she saw modern men, reenactors they were called, dressed up as Wyatt Earp, Doc Holliday, or Curly Bill. They seemed to live their role rather than just dressing up like those gunfighters from the days long gone, and Cheryl wondered to what extent they confused the historical re-enactment with reality.

She had visited the two leading saloons, Big Nose Kate's and the famous Chrystal Palace, a couple of times and liked their atmosphere but avoided the premises during the weekends. Too many drunks tried to get "funny" with her—obnoxious, really. She was seen as the new kid in town, and quite a few tried to hit on her. But none of the men fascinated Cheryl. She preferred educated men and, if possible, good looking or at least well dressed. And there was something else. Cheryl had a taste for long, wavy hair. She didn't know where that preference came from, but she had always had it as long as she could remember.

Nowadays, it seemed that most men sported a military like haircut, or even shaved heads, very much to Cheryl's distaste. She could daydream for hours about the long hair of a secret lover caressing her naked skin.

She quickly shook off the romantic thoughts. It was time to close the museum for the day. Cheryl had decided to take an evening stroll around the area that had once been known as the red-light district in the old days.

She had done a fair amount of reading lately and, for some reason, was fascinated by the past and stories about the shady ladies in this town. Students in her program had to write a long essay to graduate, so she decided to write about the topic of the fallen angels of Tombstone. Dorothea had generously lent her a whole stack of books about the soiled doves which could be well used for her studies.

Cheryl had become close friends with the McEntire couple. Despite the age difference, she liked both of them very much for their wit, humor, and high level of education. Sometimes they met for a relaxed evening of barbecuing together and enjoyed long conversations over every possible topic that crossed their minds.

Well, maybe being assigned to the Tombstone outpost isn't that bad after all, she thought while sitting on her porch, enjoying a sandwich made with fresh-sliced turkey. She emptied her glass of homemade lemonade and got up to put her plate and glass in the sink. On the way outside she grabbed her cozy wool shawl and left the house. She knew once the sun set at this higher elevation it would get chilly pretty fast.

It was different to walk the streets of Tombstone at twilight. Cheryl strolled much slower and at a more leisurely pace than her normal sporty stride. As she passed Sixth Street where the red-light district's center used to be in the old days, the sudden aroma of cherry cigars filled the air. Cheryl looked over her shoulder, but nobody was there.

Must have been from a person walking along this street before me. Cheryl inhaled deeply and immediately liked the cherry flavored tobacco, although she had never smoked her entire life. It had a pleasant aroma and seemed somewhat familiar. Strangely, as she continued to walk, the cigar smell seemed to follow her.

Probably my nose starting to play funny games because of all the mesquite bushes around here. Cheryl had heard that many people developed some sort of allergies in the desert and its fauna.

She walked by a building on the left and decided to cut over to Allen Street, as the small road ahead of her seemed to be leading right into the dusty hills outside of Tombstone's town limits. Cheryl turned left and walked by an adobe building she did not know.

A sudden pain made her groan. It was like the stab of a knife at her temples, and when she closed her eyes, green sparks appeared behind her closed eyelids. She started to feel dizzy and had to touch the wall next to her to steady herself. A weird tingle spread from her fingertips, and the hand touching the wall went numb. The smell of cherry cigars was almost overwhelming now, but nobody stood close by, and no smoke was visible.

Feeling worse by the minute, Cheryl was afraid she was going to faint.

"Mae, my sunshine. Mae!"

She recognized the voice from the other night on her porch. The numbness in her hand spread further up her arm, but she was unable to pull back her hand. "What in the world...?"

"Miss, are you okay? Can I help you?"

A young biker walked reluctantly toward her and studied her pale face. "Are you drunk?" he asked, not hiding the dismay in his voice. But then he saw the perspiration covering her face and that she was pale as a ghost despite her summer tan. It was obvious that something was wrong with Cheryl, so the young man came closer and touched her arm gently, just in time to catch her as she fainted.

"Probably dehydrated," he mumbled while he carried her toward a bench on the opposite side of the main boardwalk. He removed a water bottle from his backpack and poured some cool water into his palm to refresh her sweaty face.

She woke, feeling confused. "Where am I?"

"You fainted. I'd better take you to your hotel or wherever you're staying. Do you need a doctor?"

She shook her head. "No, thank you. I'm feeling better already. Just don't know what happened."

"Okay. I'll walk you back to your place to make sure you don't fall or faint again. It will be dark in a few minutes anyway." Cheryl nodded and thanked the man.

Behind the wall of the adobe structure, an angry scream erupted into the darkness of the building. "She's mine. I will bring her back!"

A dark shape of a pale woman held out a silver dollar coin toward the direction of the angry voice. Her blood red lipstick emphasized the grotesque mask her face had turned into. The inhabitants of the building had given her a new name. She was "Silver Dollar Elisabeth" now.

But Cheryl was unaware of all this as she thanked the stranger who walked her home. She offered him some lemonade, but he refused.

"Time to hit the road with the bike, getting dark pretty fast. By the way, my name is Morgan."

"Thank you, Morgan. I really appreciate your help. I don't know what came over me. Normally I don't have any health problems."

"Hope you feel better tomorrow. If you are still around for a while, say hi. I work at the Four Deuces Saloon down the road if you feel like stopping by."

"I definitely will. I work at the Courthouse as a trainee for the next few weeks. See you around town then."

She waved goodbye as he walked down the road toward the saloon where she assumed he most likely had parked his motorcycle.

He looks sad, head hanging down. Nice fellow. Attractive, too. The poor guy must be depressed about something.

Cheryl had no clue what had happened during her walk uptown. The sudden migraine was gone just as fast as it had appeared, and the numbness in her arm had disappeared, too. *How weird.* She sat on her rocking chair sipping her second glass of lemonade, trying to rest. Cheryl felt tired, her legs were still somewhat wobbly, and she decided to call it an early night and get some sleep.

As she turned toward the front door, the faint smell of cherry cigars caressed her nostrils again. *I must be imagining things. Just exhausted, I guess.* She went inside and headed for bed.

Curls of cigar smoke rose into the cool night air as a dark shadow leaned against the pole on Cheryl's front porch while the woman slept soundly and dreamlessly in her beautiful Victorian iron framed bed on the other side of the wall.

CHAPTER 8

A VISIT FROM THE SHERIFF

The next morning an ongoing police search was the talk of the town when Cheryl arrived at the museum. She felt refreshed from a good night's rest and decided to buy some migraine medication at the Dollar Store later, in case yesterday's headache should return. When Cheryl saw the sheriff and two Arizona rangers talking with the McEntires, she walked toward them, wondering what the fuss was all about.

The sheriff tipped his hat.

"Good morning, ma'am. May we ask you some questions?"

Cheryl looked puzzled, wondering what this was all about and shrugged her shoulders.

"Sure, go ahead."

One of the rangers unfolded a print of a woman in her early thirties with blond hair and heavy makeup. "Have you seen this lady in the past few days?" the sheriff asked.

Cheryl thought the face looked familiar. After a minute she knew where she had seen her. "I saw her at Big Nose Kate's Saloon a few days ago. She is a waitress, isn't she? What's the matter?"

One of the rangers gave her a sheriff's office business card. "Her name is Lisa Callaghan. She's missing, but her car is still parked in town. She disappeared without a trace three days ago after her evening shift. If you see or hear anything from her, let us know please."

"Disappeared you say?" A cold chill caused Cheryl to rub her arms. It was surely not the kind of news one would expect in a small town like Tombstone.

"Maybe she ran off with a handsome guy?"

The sheriff shook his head at that suggestion. "No way. She's Morgan's girlfriend. The guy who bartends at the Four Deuces. He has looked all over Cochise County for her and is mighty worried. They were planning to get married in two months. No, Lisa would not run away with some other fellow. She might be grumpy from time to time but is head over heels for Morgan, and, as far as I know, he's madly in love with her, too. We questioned him already. He's devastated and has no clue as to her whereabouts."

Cheryl remembered the sad expression on the young guy's face yesterday. *No wonder he seemed so depressed if his girlfriend had disappeared. But where in the world would she go?* Cheryl walked into the Courthouse Museum lost in thoughts.

Lisa remained the main topic for the gossip in town for a few days. Some assumed she had run away with some other cowboy, maybe chickening out of the wedding. Some thought that Morgan had something to do with her disappearance.

Just as the local authorities were about to give up the search for Lisa, her car keys were found close to her car behind the Bird Cage. Now the talk about the presumed crime scared not only some of the tourists when they heard about it, but many female locals as well. A few of them even questioned if it was safe to walk the streets of Tombstone at night.

As Cheryl and Dorothea enjoyed their Mexican dinner at

Margarita's Restaurant, Dorothea seemed thoughtful and more silent than usual. Cheryl asked if something was wrong, and after a brief hesitation, her new friend spoke, her voice barely a whisper.

"You know, Lisa is not the first woman to have disappeared in this town."

"What do you mean?" Cheryl asked, setting her fork down.

"Well, I did a lot of research on the town's history, partly for the museum and partly out of my own personal interest.

I came across similar stories of women who had disappeared in Tombstone throughout the past few decades. Some were not taken seriously, as some of the women had... had... well, let's say, a less-than-spotless reputation. So far, there are three ladies missing, including Lisa. Three women who vanished into thin air. The police were never able to press charges, as they never found any bodies or evidence of a crime, but, hell, this whole area is full of mining shafts. It would not be a difficult task at all to have a corpse disappear for good without leaving a trace."

Cheryl was shocked. She might've expected such stories in L.A. but not here in a small Western community in such a remote location. Dorothea studied the food on her plate for a few moments. When she spoke again, her voice was sad.

"What I found out is that the women started disappearing after the mines closed along with the boomtown entertainment such as the Bird Cage Brothel and Saloon in 1889. That was right after the heyday of the silver boom. First, I thought it might be one man repeatedly kidnapping girls, but there are many years between the incidents, so it can hardly be one guy responsible for all of the crimes. He would have to be as old as Methuselah. The women vanished within a time period of over a hundred and thirty years and the sad part is, as long as there's no evidence and no skeletons, the police and the FBI wouldn't follow the few facts they have. The cases are closed, or at least became 'cold,' and nobody was interested enough to solve that mystery."

Dorothea took a few bites, and her face looked thoughtful. Cheryl remained silent, sensing that there was more to it.

"They didn't find any traces of the women after they vanished, but they all have one thing in common," Dorothea said. "All of them worked in Tombstone saloons and all disappeared between late evening and twilight of the next morning."

Chills ran up and down Cheryl's spine, and she sat stone-faced. Was it possible? Was the touristy Western heritage town really the seat of such crime?

Cheryl decided to do some research to find out more about Tombstone's earlier history after the famous gunfight at the O.K. Corral. She would start at the only place she had not visited yet, the Bird Cage Theatre itself.

CHAPTER 9

THE FIRST VISIT

Scheduled to be off work the following day, Cheryl decided to pay a visit to the tourist attraction, now a well-known museum and must-see spot, according to most townsfolk. She decided to go right after breakfast, as she wanted to avoid the tourist crowds and have a look undisturbed. All Cheryl knew about the place was that it had been a brothel, a saloon and gambling establishment more than a theatre, and not a family entertainment place as it might have been in modern times.

A memory flashed of how she had fainted behind the building which she now knew to have been the Bird Cage Theatre only a few days before. This time she was prepared with a bottle of water and candy bar in her purse. *Maybe it was just a problem of low blood sugar that day.*

The lady at the front entrance who ran the day shift gave her a friendly greeting. "Hey, so finally you come to visit our museum. Welcome! I'm Heather." Apparently, the news about Cheryl working at the Courthouse Museum must have travelled fast around town.

"I'm Cheryl. Pleasure to meet you, Heather."

"Well, let me know if you need any information. I haven't started the cash register yet, but I'll give you a free ticket today. After all, you may be able to promote us among the courthouse visitors. You know how it is, one hand washes the other, and we could all use more visitors lately."

"That's very kind of you. I will most likely come back with lots of questions for my studies. And of course, I'll tell people about the famous Bird Cage Theatre."

"Feel free to ask as much as you want, sweetie." Heather handed Cheryl a ticket while pointing the way into the museum room. "You will walk through the main theatre with its stage. Then the tour takes you to the backstage area and downstairs to where the high-stake poker games took place. You will have to leave the museum through the gift shop in the basement. Once you are done with the tour walk back in here through the main entrance, and I can answer questions if you have any."

The early visitor thanked Heather, remained in the front room for a few minutes, and marveled at the beautifully tooled bar made from a dark hardwood and the mirror behind it with the shelves full of antique liquor bottles. A small staircase at the other end of the room led upstairs to a gallery under the wooden ceiling of the theatre. She slowly walked toward the well-worn steps and suddenly shivered as though something, or someone, was holding her back from moving any closer.

"These were the stairs leading up to the so-called cribs. The girls would go up there to entertain quite differently than the girls on the stage, if you know what I mean." Heather laughed and winked. "Actually, it was cheap money up there, mainly dirty miners and sweaty cowboys looking for some female affection. The ones that were better off had the pleasure of booking the beautiful women in the downstairs brothel."

Cheryl stared at the museum's employee. "You mean there were different classes of prostitutes?"

Heather nodded. "Oh, yes, dear. The ones who were young, pretty, and smart actually could earn a fortune as soiled doves in Tombstone. But the older ones or the unattractive ones, the Chinese or Mexican prostitutes were often abused and had to serve male needs for very low pay. Most of them either fell sick with diseases or committed suicide by drinking poison. But, as I said, some were almost like movie stars of today and earned big bucks."

Cheryl was fascinated and looked around at all the items in the saloon entry area. She saw some sort of an antique music box with the mechanical metal plate of Silent Night still resting on its mechanism. To Cheryl's surprise the music box came all the way from Germany and would have played the famous Christmas Carol if it still functioned. A big oil painting of an exotic dancer with three breasts covered the bigger part of the wall next to the stairs that led to the cribs. Cheryl studied the piece of art. "Why in the world does she have three breasts?"

Heather pointed at the picture. "Meet Fatima also called Little Egypt. She was indeed a belly dancer who performed here in the old days. If she really had three breasts, I can't say. We never found proof of it. But she was a living performer at our establishment. See the three holes in the canvas? Some rowdy cowboys must have used her portrait for target practicing with their knives. One thing is sure, this town has seen a lot of strange things since its founding."

Cheryl thanked Heather and turned to the door leading to the main museum room. Stepping through the tiny doorway, she noticed how dark and cool it was behind the plywood wall which separated the bar area from the theatre section. When the door closed behind her, she felt as if she was being swallowed into the vacuum of a long-forgotten time. Cheryl glanced around but didn't know where to begin.

On the other side of the room, she saw a stage framed with an old, dusty curtain, its golden fringes dangling. The burgundy velvet material was faded and held none of its original bold color as it hung sadly from the high ceiling as if it were tired of the years gone by. An old piano stood in front of the stage like a silent witness waiting to be played. Below the high ceiling numerous "cribs" faced the stage and the center of the room from both sides. The cribs were compact chambers sparsely furnished with a simple bed and a faded blanket. A petroleum lamp once provided a dim light. There was barely enough space to walk around the small cot, but the miners must not have cared about that.

The museum had installed small spotlights in the upstairs cribs which illuminated the wallpaper that sported a rich ornamental design with different flowers. Some of it had started to peel off the walls, and the stains of rainwater entering the building through the ceiling explained why the walls were damaged in more than one of the cribs. Dusty velvet curtains hung on either side of each little private loge. They would have provided a bit of privacy whenever the crib was occupied by a soiled dove and her customer.

As Cheryl looked up at the painted wooden ceiling, she noticed countless holes. *My God, those must be bullet holes.* Her brain conjured an image of people wildly shooting at each other and toward the ceiling, maybe to let off drunken steam. *That must have been insane! How could they have taken such a risk in a crowded room, especially with people being upstairs?*

Shaking her head in disbelief, she wandered slowly from one showcase to the next studying the objects in them. The variety of beautiful items was impressive—from medical instruments to porcelain plates, silver cutlery, and even old gambling tables and a pool table. The room was full of different artifacts. Clothes, old music instruments, and guns—all of them whispered of the old days and their heroes and villains.

There was a faro table that had been used by the notorious Doc Holliday himself if one wanted to believe the printed sign next to it. In a side niche she even saw a displayed dentist chair. Cheryl moved steadily toward the piano in the center of the room. She softly pressed one of the keys. A faint, mistuned tone sounded. The keys felt strange, and she sensed a tingle as if the piano were caressing her back. Cheryl quickly pulled back her hand, which had grown cold.

To her left was a narrow staircase leading behind the stage. A small booth next to the stairs, the only one at base level, housed a little table, a single wooden chair, a deck of poker cards, and a bottle of whiskey, all seemingly waiting for the next person willing to gamble. Cheryl closed her eyes, as all of a sudden, the scent of cherry cigar smoke engulfed her.

When she opened her eyes again, she still stood in front of the piano, yet, by God, the place was not the same. It was loud, and smoke drifted in thick layers through the room causing her eyes to burn. The whole place was crowded with people, mostly men in frontier-styled clothes. "My God, where did all these people come from?" Cheryl whispered. The air bore the stench of sweat, alcohol, and the sulfur smell of gun powder. The piano played a lively polka song, and the establishment bustled with the noise of cheerful female laughter and husky male voices. The clinking of glasses from men toasting each other rang in her ears. A singing voice accompanied the piano. Cheryl looked at the entertainer who wore a daring, low-cut, red dress with a big bustle emphasizing her backside.

She stared at the woman whose hair was pinned up with beautiful ivory combs. Her face had been powdered a ghostly white, her cheeks and lips colored red. The fact that Cheryl was able to see the dusty curtain of the stage shimmering through the lady's body made her skin crawl with fear.

What in the world is happening to me? Since when do I suffer from hallucinations? She knew she had entered the room alone, but now it was packed with folks in strange attire. Cheryl panicked not knowing what went on. She intended to leave the museum right away, and the closest way to escape from the crowd were the stairs right next to her. When she turned her head away from the stage toward the single poker booth she stared right into his face. Long, light brown hair fell over his broad shoulders, and his well-trimmed mustache almost hid the curve of his smiling lips as he looked at her, his steely gray-blue eyes showing an amused twinkle.

"Hello, Mae. Finally, you are here again, my love. I have waited so long for you."

Cheryl didn't feel the impact of the hardwood floor in front of the poker booth. She was unconscious before she struck it.

CHAPTER 10

MAE DAVENPORT ARRIVES

*J*anuary 1882, Tombstone, Arizona territory

MAE GOT OFF THE STAGECOACH. Oh, how she hated to travel these god-forsaken dirt trails on the stage lines.

Not only was this dangerous territory packed with outlaws and renegade Apache, but chances were high to break every dang bone in one's body because of the stage's constant and wild jolting up and down and back and forth. She felt as though every spot of her petite figure was bruised by the time she got off the coach. But neither she nor her friends had a choice. The carnival group with which she travelled as a singer and dancer moved from one dusty mining camp to the next, stopping wherever there was a faint chance to earn some of the silver and gold the miners dug out of Mother Earth during their backbreaking twelve-hour shifts. As Mae stumbled out of the stage onto the dusty road, she took a look around.

To her surprise, Tombstone was quite large. There were a lot of buildings along the main street, which seemed to accommodate a hell of a lot of saloons.

Well, well, generally money is spent easily where whiskey flows freely out of many barrels, she mused.

At present Tombstone was the place to be. Thousands of people hoping for the lucky strike flocked into town every month. They all planned to search for the mother lode of the precious silver in the surrounding hills.

Now all these men needed distraction from their hard work as much as they craved for food and a place to sleep. It was said the saloons in Tombstone were open throughout the full twenty-four hours of the long days, seven days a week.

The carnival group was scheduled to entertain guests at an establishment called the Bird Cage Theatre. Mae thought that was a funny name. However, that house of entertainment had achieved the reputation of being the most notorious honky-tonk in the whole Southwest. It was worth a stop on the group's tour through the frontier areas. Some even claimed that the Bird Cage Theatre was spoken of even in St. Louis thousands of miles away. Hard to believe, but then one never knew. The talk about legends travelled fast and wide distances.

After the show troop checked into a simple boarding house on Fremont Street, they didn't waste any time but quickly unpacked their costumes from their trunks and prepared for the first performance at the theatre. They were scheduled to meet the owner at the back of the building by sunset. As the carnival group arrived, they could hear the noise of the crowd flowing down the busy street.

"Looks like there's already quite a commotion going on in there," Mae's friend Peter commented. He was an expert trick shooter and well-liked wherever he had performed so far. Unfortunately, there were always some fools who tried to provoke Peter into a shooting competition, man against man. He was smart enough to avoid any kind of deadly gunfight. It would have thrown the whole troop knee deep into trouble if Peter left the group, whether due to a bullet or an angry lynch mob. Mae hoped he would be able to avoid trouble here as well, but somehow, she had her doubts. Tombstone's reputation as the town that took a man's life every day had spread far beyond Arizona's borders, and she heard a lot about it wherever they stopped for a few days. It worried her.

As Peter knocked hard against the wooden door in the rear wall of the theatre, Mae was pulled out of her deep reflections about this town. They had to wait for another quarter of an hour until the door opened and a scantily dressed woman stood in front of them. Mae was not surprised at all.

She had seen her share of prostitution all along the frontier and had begun to compare the income of the shady ladies with her own as a circus singer and dancer. It appeared that the soiled doves definitely earned a much higher income than Mae's meager wage, and she didn't like it especially when one considered the hard rehearsal which stood behind her talent.

The lady of the night asked them to follow her to the area behind the stage and sent for Bill Hutchinson, the owner of the house of ill fame. He came around the corner of the heavy stage drapes and greeted them.

"Thank God, you arrived in town just in time. It's payday for the miners, and we have a full house. You can start your show right away!" He hurried off toward the downstairs area of the building.

The group got ready, and Peter entered the stage to start his performance. One of his tricks was to hit a poker card while shooting backward over his shoulder using a mirror to help him aim. When he hit the ace right in the center, the crowd cheered frenetically.

At the end of Peter's performance, numerous gunshots erupted, and Mae, who stood behind the stage drapes, feared for her friend's safety, but Peter came jumping behind the stage, laughing like a mad man.

"This is the most notorious place I have ever seen. My goodness, it's packed to the limit. They shoot holes in the ceiling instead of cheering. Let's hope they don't put bullet holes into our bellies at the end of our performance. One thing is sure, my children, we can earn a lot of silver here in this dusty town of Tombstone! You wouldn't believe it but they even throw silver dollars onto the stage." Mae didn't know if she should be scared or enthusiastic like Peter was.

The show went on. At last, it was Mae's turn on stage to perform her ballet dancing act. She usually sang a tune or two first since the dance was strenuous and left her with barely any breath for singing. As she entered the stage, she was shocked when she saw the crowd.

The room was packed and the cigar smoke so thick she couldn't make out the faces in the back near the bar. The upstairs cribs were filled with men and soiled doves, and a few curtains were closed. In front of the stage all the tables were occupied with drinking prospectors. They appeared rough and dusty but willing to spend their week's earnings.

Various girls in daring dresses no decent town lady would have ever worn sat on their laps or moved swiftly from table to table with baskets full of beverages. Some of the girls climbed toward the upstairs cribs with miners quickly following them scrambling up the stairs.

Mae bent down to the young Irish piano player and tried to make herself heard. She asked him to tinkle a well-known tune. At the beginning her voice was barely heard above the noise, but slowly, heads started turning toward the stage. More than one miner's attention was caught by the crystal-clear tone of this beauty's voice.

When Mae turned to the right, she saw him sitting in the first booth next to the stage. He played poker with another man. His hair was long, light brown and wavy, his mustache short and well-trimmed. His gray-blue eyes and high cheek bones added to his handsome features. The man looked somewhat exotic, and his calm posture seemed out of place in the rowdy crowd. He didn't pay attention to her on the stage or to what was going on around him. Instead, he concentrated on the deck of cards in his hand, his face cast in a serious expression. His opponent was a cowboy wearing a pistol holster around his lean hips. His black hair was partly covered by a hat he had pushed back. Mae didn't see the man's face as he sat with his back to the stage, but the more she looked, the more she was impressed by the handsome features of the long-haired gambler.

As she finished her song, she earned a fair amount of applause. "So far so good," she mumbled.

One of the carnival group members took the stage with her violin and started playing a Hungarian folksong. Now that there were two good looking women on stage, the men in the audience paid much more attention to what was happening. They likely expected another song from Mae because when she began dancing a daring ballet choreography, blank surprise showed on many faces in front of the stage.

It didn't take long for the prospectors, saddle tramps, and gamblers to get on their feet in order to get a better glimpse of the beautiful, extremely flexible woman who could assume positions that fueled every man's fantasies. The audience cheered and clapped enthusiastically.

When the Hungarian song rose from a single violin, the handsome gambler known in Tombstone under the name of Russian Bill looked up. His face conveyed an appreciation and longing for the music of his beloved Russian homeland that he often spoke about to his friends. Both the woman playing the violin and the beautiful dancer held his interest. He glimpsed at the crowd, and it was obvious that the two beauties on the stage were the reason why men were on their feet pushing and shoving against the edge of the stage.

His friend Curly Bill, whom he played poker with every night, had told him about the arrival of a new carnival troop earlier that evening, but Russian Bill had told Curly Bill that he wasn't interested in circus, women, or whatsoever. He was known for having his mind set on gambling, and in case he was in need of a woman, he was always welcomed in the more luxurious bordellos around town. A rich, handsome man was never denied anything in the red-light district of this mining camp. "The new traveling carnival group holds no appeal for me." He waved his friends comment about the group off. However, that seemed to change when he heard the folk song.

The girl on stage whirled around like a dust devil and leaped into a daring classical ballet position.

She turned her face toward his table and flashed him a dazzling smile. Single strands of her dark hair stuck to her sweaty forehead, and her cheeks flamed red from her performance, as she panted hard.

The good-looking Russian stared at her breasts held tightly by the costume and saw how they rose and fell while she tried to catch her breath. When she got up and bowed in front of the crowd almost everybody in the theatre was clapping. Some of old Bill Clanton's cowboys were shooting at the ceiling, which made her jump for a moment. But she waved and smiled at them and quickly ran behind the stage curtain.

"They loved you, darling," Peter exclaimed.

Mae smiled at him. She was tired from traveling to Tombstone and having to perform right away.

Peter told her that they would perform again the following day. Obviously, the owner appreciated their act and asked them to stay at least two weeks. That meant guaranteed income, so they all happily agreed and left the premises to rest after their work and travels.

Meanwhile, on the other side of the stage, Russian Bill watched her leave as he turned the cherry flavored cigar between his fingers. Curly Bill slapped his shoulders, jolting him from his thoughts.

"What's wrong, my Russian prince? Did the little dancing devil impress you so much that you reject your poker game?" A knowing smile curled Curly Bill's lips.

Bill shook his head and gazed at his cards again concentrating on his next move. He smiled at Curly Bill for calling him "Russian prince." After all, that was what he really was although hardly anyone believed his stories. Russian Bill couldn't be called a prince but a nobleman indeed, and it was a fact that he was quite wealthy. Although he concentrated on his cards again, Curly Bill caught his friend more than once glancing at the stage where the mysterious, beautiful dancer had performed less than half an hour ago.

"Should I ask around who she is?" Curly Bill mocked his friend.

Russian Bill shook his head. "Reckon we will find out soon enough."

CHAPTER 11

MAE'S NEW FRIEND

The next two weeks of performing at the theatre passed so quickly Mae was barely aware of the days. Tombstone had cast its spell on the beautiful young woman as on thousands of others who flocked into town every month. During the day, the dusty streets were busy with crowds of mineworkers, cow hands, storekeepers, and stagecoaches that rattled into town from Benson, Bisbee, and other settlements. The air smelled of dust and horse manure.

There was some kind of trouble every day. Triggered by whiskey, opium, or bad luck in gambling, violent fights erupted daily and often came to a deadly end for one of the opponents.

Sometimes a heated discussion about a deck of poker cards or the favors of a painted cat were enough to get a man killed on the busy streets. Most fights erupted right inside the saloons, and a scary number of men looking for some entertainment died in them simply for being at the wrong place the wrong time. The undertakers were mighty busy and earned a fortune. Yet despite all the dangers one could encounter in a pioneer town, Tombstone's atmosphere sizzled with the hope to strike it rich and the unbreakable will of folks to create a better tomorrow for themselves.

The red-light district was the largest Mae had seen on her travels so far. She had become friends with Lizette, an exceptional beauty with copper colored hair that fell in wild curls across her back all the way to her shapely derriere. Her skin had a white, creamy tone, and hundreds of freckles added to her girlish beauty. Lizette worked at the Bird Cage Theatre as the so-called "Flying Nymph," using her trapeze performance to attract men to follow her into her little chamber where she plied the oldest trade of the world. Mae liked Lizette a lot but was aware of the girl's unstable personality. The life as a prostitute at her young age had left traces on her soul, and God only knew what her childhood had been like.

The red-haired sporting girl was the one who suggested to Mae that she should leave the carnival and stay behind to earn much better money as an "entertaining lady." Mae still shied away from the idea of letting men touch her for money, but she was very much aware of the fortune some of the Bird Cage girls earned in Tombstone. Besides that, she would not have hesitated to forget about morals if a specific man would have showed serious interest in her.

By now she knew that the man of her innocent daydreams was called Russian Bill. At least, that was how he was known in town. She had heard that he claimed to be the son of a Russian noblewoman and must be quite wealthy, as he rented the booth next to the stage to play his poker games in the Bird Cage every evening. Holding that spot exclusively for himself cost around twenty-five dollars in silver per night, a fortune considering that it equaled the weekly prospector's pay for their hard twelve-hour shifts underground in those shafts.

Mae found out that the handsome European had many friends among a gang the town's people simply referred to as the "cowboys," and Lizette told her that Russian Bill's friend Curly Bill Brocius had a couple of heated discussions with the Earp brothers who, according to her friend, represented the law in town. "I don't trust either side," Lizette told her one day. "Those Earp brothers talk of morals, but God knows that they earn a fortune with mining and gambling. Their friend is the notorious Doc Holliday, a trunk who has nothing to lose because he is a lunger. They shot down some of the cowboys over at the livery stable. Some folks claim it was cold blooded murder and put three young fellows into their graves. Sometimes I wonder who the bigger crooks are, the cowboys who are cattle rustlers or the Earps. One thing is sure, Brocius and his friends have not forgotten the gunfight."

"Why do you think the Earps aren't trustworthy?" Mae asked Lizette over a cup of coffee in the backstage area of the Bird Cage.

"See, the Earps earn their money mainly with gambling licenses and shares in some of the mines. They will not allow others to take a piece of their cake. Plus, most of them are either married or live with sporting girls. One of the Earp wives even ran her own brothel somewhere East. So, their vest is not as white as they claim it to."

"I understand," Mae said. "It is all about the money, right?"

Lizette nodded. "Yes, and the cowboys are a gang of cattle thieves and dangerous murderers. They don't want their cattle rustling being disturbed by some law dogs coming down here from Dodge City to start their own businesses. I would not be astonished if the scene escalates again soon just like it did at the O.K. Corral. If so, blood will be shed again, I am sure."

"What about this Doc Holliday?" Mae wanted to know.

Lizette shook her head. "He is a fine gentleman. But he is sick as a dog with the coughing sickness. He will die, and he knows it, therefore he seeks for every possible fight and drinks himself to death. Sometimes it seems as if he looks for trouble on purpose hoping that some enemy would put him out of his misery."

"What about Russian Bill?" Mae asked shyly, almost biting her tongue.

Lizette smiled at her knowingly. "Ah, our beautiful Russian Prince. So far none of us has conquered his heart," she added with a sigh.

"Bill sees himself as a member of the outlaws. He is a professional gambler and pretends to be one of the dangerous boys." Mae had difficulties believing that. Behind his hard stare and rough behavior lay a well-educated gentleman with the most astonishing gray-blue eyes she had ever seen. They reminded her of the sky when one of the thunderstorms moving in from the Huachuca Mountains was turning it into a stormy gray. As far as Mae had witnessed, that man lacked the brutal, nasty behavior of such scalawags as the Clanton boys.

"He claims to be the son of a Russian noblewoman and that he had been an elite officer under the ruling czar. Sadly, nobody believes his tales," Lizette added with a shrug of her slender shoulders.

The beautiful dancer nodded as she had overheard people making fun of Bill, and it seemed that even his outlaw buckaroo friends didn't take him seriously. Mae saw them whispering behind their hands watching Russian Bill from the other side of the saloon laughing and pointing fingers at him.

CHAPTER 12

STAYING FOR RUSSIAN BILL

Mae observed Russian Bill playing his card games every night and by now had to admit that her heart skipped a beat or two whenever she saw him. She also realized that many of the girls were trying to lure him into their beds. The pretty carnival performer was not a fool and knew how dangerous it would be to make herself enemies among the ladies of the night. However, he occupied Mae's daily thoughts and in all the nights she performed at the Bird Cage Theatre, she had never witnessed Russian Bill spending the night with one of the soiled doves.

She was relieved about it, as she knew that witnessing him disappearing into one of the cribs with a girl would hurt her more than she dared to admit to anybody, including herself.

After the two weeks passed and the group's performance agreement expired, her fellow circus members were about to pack up to conquer the next boomtown. After two sleepless nights Mae took a tough decision and told Peter and the others that she would be staying behind to continue performing at the Bird Cage.

Nobody was surprised, but Peter hugged her hard, asking if she was sure about this. She nodded through tears. He had been an awesome companion and knew her heart better than anybody else among the entire group. The trick shooter pulled her aside to share fatherly advice. "Girl, I have seen the sparks of desire you feel for Russian Bill gleaming in your wonderful eyes, and I truly hope that you don't have to pay a high price for listening to your foolish heart. I have seen too many broken hearts along the trail and wish you the very best. If things go wrong, I hope you know that you always have a home in this crazy troop, my friend." Peter gently wiped away her tears and kissed her on the forehead. He had always been very fond of Mae Davenport.

Mae stood outside the boarding house and watched the stagecoach with her fellow performers on board disappearing down the hill on the road toward Benson. She felt a twinge of loneliness in her heart. *Will I ever see them again? God, I hope this was not the biggest mistake of my life,* she mused. But it was too late, and she had made up her mind. When she turned around and looked toward Allen Street, she felt how Tombstone lured her back into its center not willing to let the young woman leave.

Mae still had enough money saved from her payment as dancer and decided to stay in the lodging house for another night or two until she found a simple home.

Lizette had asked her to move in with her and another girl known as Crazy Anne. They both shared a small house, and Mae seriously considered the offer. But right now, she felt like being alone for a few days. She needed some privacy to get used to her new life and the fact that she had left the people she had been used to for over three years. Mae knew that she would miss the others dearly.

The bad part about being alone now was the fact that she had to face having no company, especially at dinnertime, until she got settled in Tombstone. The town's honorable women avoided her in the same way that they bashed every female who worked at the notorious theatre. After all, it was no secret that the establishment was more a house of ill repute where gambling, drinking, and sinful behavior was available twenty-four hours a day. All performers were outcasts in the eyes of the so-called pure women, so the ladies of easy morals would be the only possible friends Mae might have in the future.

In the early afternoon Mae decided to grab a bite at the friendliest place she had been to so far in this ruthless town. It was the small restaurant owned and run by a pretty Irish gal called Nellie Cashman. Actually, Nellie carried the nickname "angel of the miners' camp," and indeed, she was an angel—friendly and humble and always there for the needy people. Nellie didn't judge anyone and always served meals to the prostitutes. Plus, Mae was pretty convinced that no man would try to get "fresh" with her at Nellie's place. The restaurant owner had earned the equal respect of everybody, and men behaved well in her restaurant.

Mae Davenport walked over to the corner next to a huge water pump which kept the mining shafts dry. The noise created by the pump was annoying, but when she got closer to Nellie's place she could already smell the mouthwatering aroma of the well-recommended cuisine. It made up for the noise of the steam machine close by. She sat down and ordered the day's special—meatloaf, fresh potatoes, and homemade lemonade.

After taking her order Nellie tugged one of her gorgeous black curls behind her ear and gazed at Mae and in her usual straightforward manner, asked about her plans. "So, you're going to stay in Tombstone and are no longer with the carnival, is that right?"

Mae nodded and told her she would continue working at the Bird Cage Theatre. She prepared herself for the expected critical glance or public bashing, but it didn't come. Instead, Nellie Cashman sat down at her table and patted her guest's hand.

"I want you to know that the life as a soiled dove is much too dangerous to linger in it for long. Grab as much money as you can, or a decent husband, if you should ever find one in your arms. Please watch out for yourself. Get one of those small guns to hide under your skirts."

"I will continue to perform as dancer and singer. I don't consider working as a shady lady," Mae tried to defend herself, blushing deeply.

But Nellie waved her objection off. "I want you to know that you are always welcome at one of my tables, Mae Davenport. It doesn't matter what you do at the Bird Cage. The frontier is a rough terrain for a woman alone, so we ladies need to stick together." She patted Mae's hand again and got up. "Now, I better get your food off the stove. I'll be back." With a smile, she rushed off to the small kitchen at the back of the restaurant. Mae looked around with tears pooling in her eyes.

She was touched by the other woman's humble words. Nellie Cashman had indeed called her a lady. What an astonishing human being she was. Slowly but surely, Mae understood why Nellie was called the angel of the camp. Not only did she look gorgeous with her delicate features, lush, curly hair, and gentle eyes but she also seemed to be the humblest person.

CHAPTER 13

MEETING BILL

"She's a great person, isn't she?" A low voice with a foreign accent and a soft timbre next to her made her jump. Russian Bill stood right beside her table. She had not seen him approach, and now here he was, his head slightly bowed in greeting. Mae had never spoken to him before. The impact of hearing his voice was astonishing. She felt like a hundred butterflies were whirling around in her stomach.

The unexpected visitor softly touched the back of the second chair.

"May I?" he asked.

Mae nodded slowly, still too surprised about meeting him here and slightly annoyed with herself over the fact that her cheeks felt flushed and hot.

"May I introduce myself officially? I am William Tattenbaum, but everyone calls me Russian Bill. And you are?"

Finally, she found her voice again and answered with a shy smile. "Mae Davenport, known as Mae Davenport."

He smiled about her obvious sense of humor. "Actually, you

are wrong about that, Miss Davenport. At the Bird Cage you are already known as the "Dancing Fawn."

She stared at him, her cheeks even redder. "Are you teasing me, sir?"

"Call me Bill, please, and it is true. They call you a dancing fawn due to your huge dark eyes and, forgive me for being so blunt, also due to your shapely legs, which are exposed for everyone's pleasure each time you dance." Mae stared at the tablecloth, embarrassed over the comment about her legs.

"No reason to feel ashamed, Miss Davenport. You are indeed a beauty, one of God's finer creations."

The sound of his voice made her shiver. Hearing it felt like a tender touch, and it left a tingle crawling up and down her spine.

Mae was glad to see Nellie walking over with a plate of steaming food because she felt as if she might faint at any minute. This man honestly confused her. He was a gambler, perhaps an outlaw, yet he spoke with the highest manners and dignity. It was clear that William Tattenbaum was an educated man. Maybe the rumors about him being a nobleman were not false after all. There was something about the way he behaved, his wardrobe and the proud way he held his head, which told Mae that he did not fit into the general crowd of a mining camp.

Nellie looked at Bill. "Howdy, Bill. Did you drop your cards for the sake of one of my decent lunches?"

"Actually, that is indeed the case, Miss Nellie. You know I cannot resist your meatloaf. It is much too delicious."

"So, I reckon I will bring you a plate with it and your beloved hash browns and gravy to go with it, right? Where will you sit?" she asked with a broad smile.

The gambler glanced at Mae, a trace of unexpected uncertainty showing on his prominent features. Mae nodded and mumbled, "You can eat at my table, of course. I don't fancy eating alone, anyway."

"Very well, then," said Nellie and returned to her kitchen.

"Thank you, Miss Davenport."

"Call me Mae, please."

"If you don't mind, then Mae it will be." He pointed to her plate, and she started to eat. The food was delicious.

Russian Bill studied her face for a moment. When he spoke again, he looked a bit concerned. "I heard you decided to stay here to continue performing at the Bird Cage. Is that true?"

"Looks like news travels fast in this town," she answered with a broad grin.

He nodded. "That is true. I hope you are aware that you are going to encounter dangerous situations in the future. The life of a fallen angel can be prosperous, yet deadly, too, Mae."

She blushed again and put down her fork. She was clearly embarrassed. He knew better than she that her new performing arrangement did not only include dancing and singing.

"Please, don't misunderstand me, my dear. I accept your decision. This is your life. Who am I to judge you? I am a gambler, and people don't consider me a gentleman of morals either. I just want you to be aware of the dangers. I also want you to know that you can count on me as a friend if you should ever need any help."

The shy dancer was completely taken by surprise and asked him bluntly how she deserved such an offer after he heard what she was going to soon become. William Tattenbaum looked deeply into her eyes.

"Mae, I come from a country far away and often miss it. You could say that I even feel homesick, but for reasons I want to keep to myself I cannot return. But when I watch and listen to your performance, you literally bring me back to my home soil. It warms my heart, and I'm less lonely. It almost feels as if my family is around me, although I am sure that I will never see them again. As a matter of fact, I feel close to them when I hear you sing and watch you doing the Hungarian gypsy dance. By now I don't doubt anymore that one can find a home in another person."

Mae stared at him. She was speechless. That was likely the most beautiful thing anyone had ever told her about her performance, and it touched her heart deeply. She knew the dark hours of loneliness far too well. Mae Davenport also had to leave her family behind. Her parents and siblings had banned her from their fancy home where she grew up on the East Coast. When her family discovered she wanted to become a singer and dancer, they had tried to shatter her dreams and wishes for independence by plotting to marry her to an old business partner of her father's. When she refused to do so, they locked her in her room for weeks, feeding her through a slide in the door like a prisoner. One day she managed to escape, knowing she would never see her family again. It broke her heart, but the call for freedom had been too strong to resist.

Russian Bill touched her elbow gently. She shook off the unpleasant thoughts of the past and looked at him. A silent understanding passed between them that told each of them had constantly battled the same ghosts of their past.

They ate their meal in silence, but it was pleasant. When Nellie came to clear the table, the handsome gambler gave her enough coins to settle the bill for both of them. He hushed Mae's protest with a single fingertip to his sensually shaped lips. "It was a true pleasure for me, Mae, so paying for your meal is the least I can do."

Mae returned to the theatre the same evening. She felt awkward being there without her troop of carnival performers but faced it as bravely as possible. William Tattenbaum sat in his booth as usual, handing out a deck of cards to one of the cowboy friends of Curly Bill, and greeted her warmly. She smiled at him and walked on stage to get ready for her first song.

CHAPTER 14

VISIONS AT THE BIRD CAGE

Someone gently slapped her face.

"Hey there, wake up, will you."

Cheryl slowly opened her eyes and looked straight into Heather's face. Things were still blurry, and she didn't know where she was. Slowly, she turned her head. She carefully touched the bump which had started to form on her forehead. "What in the world...?" She had a severe headache. *I must have hit the banister on the small stairs next to the stage.* As she tried to get up from the floor, Heather helped her to her feet. Cheryl stood on wobbly legs and looked around confused. *Where the heck am I,* she wondered, but then she remembered visiting the Bird Cage Theatre.

"What happened, girl?" Heather wanted to know.

Cheryl shook her head. "I have no idea. I wanted to walk behind the stage, but I fell, and I don't remember anything after that."

"Let's go to the front. I have some water. Tell you what, you can finish your tour another day when you feel better. Maybe you're not used to the altitude here."

Cheryl looked at Heather. It seemed as if the museum employee was nervous. If Cheryl hadn't known better, she would have thought Heather wanted to get rid of her.

Cheryl waited a little while, drinking some of the offered water and watching Heather selling some tickets to a group of visitors. When Cheryl felt better, she agreed to come by on her next day off to explore the rest of the artifacts.

At home, the confused woman had brewed some coffee, but the mug sat on the small table next to her, untouched.

What's happening to me? Dang, this is the second time I fainted within a few days. I wonder if I am getting seriously ill. Maybe I should get a checkup at the Sierra Vista hospital? I'll ask Dorothea to recommend a good doctor.

Closing her eyes, she touched the mug absently. Her thoughts returned to the Bird Cage Theatre. She had never been there before that day, but the place seemed so familiar to her. It was truly bewildering. She had felt at peace there, almost as if every corner of the building welcomed her.

She shook her head at this thought. Cheryl smelled the rich flavor of the coffee, yet there was another scent that still lingered in her nose as well. It was the smooth aroma of cherry cigars, but Cheryl could not explain where it came from.

The next few days she worked at the Courthouse Museum but seemed to be preoccupied from time to time as she reviewed the weird visit to the historic theatre, feeling foolish at the same time for doing so. Dorothea started to get concerned and asked Cheryl if everything was all right.

"Everything is just fine. I think the long hours of studying in the evenings are starting to take their toll."

But her superior's face showed a knowing expression.

"Remember when I said that Tombstone has a way of sharing its history with a small number of people in a very special way?"

Cheryl waited without answering but recalled the conversation. Dorothea's face bore a serious expression. "I wouldn't be astonished if you are one of those rare people to whom Tombstone really speaks."

"What do you mean? I don't get it."

Her elder friend gently rotated the glass she held between her fingers, 'round and 'round, trying to find the right words. "I know this may sound nutty or just plain silly, but some people, including me by the way, see things in Tombstone that cannot be explained by science or books. There are haunted areas here, and the Bird Cage is known to be a hotspot for such activities. So, don't be shocked in case you start to see weird things around you."

Cheryl laughed out loud. "Wait a minute. Are you saying there are ghosts in Tombstone and that you've actually seen them yourself?"

"Sure, sounds crazy, but I know what I've seen since we moved here."

"I don't know what to say. You're talking ghosts and spirits."

There was that voice I heard on the porch. No one was around. And what about the smell of cherry cigars? Every time I smell it there is not a single soul with a cigar around me. Is it really possible that restless souls from the Old West haunt this town?

Dorothea touched her hand. "Take your time to think about this. Whenever you're ready, I'll tell you what I've experienced since we have been living here. One thing I can assure you of, I know my great-grandmother pretty well by now due to the paranormal side of Tombstone."

The museum manager continued with her chores while Cheryl remained seated for a moment lost in thought.

Maybe they're playing a trick on me. After all, I am the new girl and all that. Ghosts? How silly. Yet a tiny flame of curiosity had started to lick at Cheryl's subconscious.

CHAPTER 15

WHO IS MAE DAVENPORT

*H*er next day off was a sunny Wednesday, beautiful with crisp, cool air. *Maybe another trip to the Bird Cage? Use my free ticket to explore the rest of the building? Or rather, should I stay away from that place?*

Drinking a strong cup of the Arbuckle coffee that Bert had gotten her hooked on, she watched two red cardinal birds hopping from one branch of the rose bush to another. Cheryl decided she was much too curious to let the opportunity slip by, so she dressed in jeans and a white blouse and walked briskly to the upper part of the tourist area and straight to the old adobe structure.

Heather wasn't there, and Cheryl was relieved, embarrassed by what had happened during her last visit. She had never liked being the center of attention.

The attractive woman explained who she was to the lady behind the entrance counter. "I wasn't able to finish the tour on my last visit." She pulled out the used free admission ticket from her hip pocket.

"Oh, you're the gal working at the courthouse, right? Heather told me to let you in for free if you came by."

"Thanks so much." I wonder if Heather told her I kind of fainted.

"Feel free to come back to the front room if you have any questions after strolling through the entire place. Otherwise, the tour leads through the gift store to the side exit next to the parking lot," the lady said, then opened the door to the main theatre for her.

Cheryl walked into the dark room, cautiously taking each step. The cribs on the second floor stared down like the cold eyes of a stranger. Her skin immediately developed goosebumps after setting foot into the main room.

I won't touch the piano this time.

She walked quickly by the poker booth and hurriedly climbed the small stairs entering the section behind the curtain. She didn't want to risk another spell of dizziness in front of the stage. However, she turned her head on an impulse, scared to see folks dressed up as pioneers again, but the room was empty except for the hundreds of artifacts.

The sudden sight of swirling smoke surprised her. It drifted out of the poker booth which had been occupied by a gambler named Russian Bill according to the hand painted sign next to the stairs leading behind the stage. "I thought smoking was prohibited in the entire building," she mumbled while she stared at the swirls of cigar smoke curling against the ceiling of the booth.

Where does that smoke come from? And I can't remember the deck of cards with the queen of hearts next to the empty whiskey bottle. Was it there when I last visited?

Cheryl turned and walked into the backstage area. Somehow standing behind the stage curtain made her happy. She didn't know why, but she felt like stepping onto the stage to dance and sing. Joy swept through her. At least, until she turned around and looked straight at the black- and gold-colored hearse standing in the far corner about twenty feet behind the stage. The vehicle lured there like a scary messenger of death.

By now she had heard people talk about the "Black Moriah," the hearse for the last journey of the dead to Tombstone's Boot Hill. Yet standing next to it was a different story. It made her skin crawl with fear. She could sense the dead who had been transported to the cemetery with it. Cheryl knew instantly that this was not one of the many Tombstone movie props that were displayed throughout the entire town. No, this was the real deal. The dead bodies of unfortunate victims of the notorious past had travelled in this piece of ghostly, yet beautifully crafted horse-drawn carriage. It was trimmed with real Tombstone silver and sheet gold, which gave it a precious and dignified look.

A small child's coffin leaned against the wheel of the hearse and nearly brought Cheryl to tears. She shivered and wanted to leave. *Right now!* The frightened woman didn't want to imagine a small, innocent child resting on the faded linen inside the tiny wooden coffin, but the picture forced itself into her consciousness. She could hardly stand the thought of a mother weeping over that casket and considered returning to the main entrance to leave.

"Mae, come to me, please."

Out of the blue there it was again, the soothing low voice she had heard days before. It stopped her from leaving, and Cheryl turned toward the sound of it.

"Mae, I am waiting for you. Come to me!"

She was not aware of setting one foot in front of the other, slowly walking toward another staircase at the rear wall leading downstairs into the building's basement and further into the past of the Bird Cage Theatre.

She touched the adobe wall to her right, and with each careful step she drew closer to the strong smell of the cigar, which increased in intensity the closer she came to the basement. Cheryl heard the clinking of whiskey glasses and the jingle of coins being thrown on top of each other among the shuffling sound of poker cards—and she had no explanation why these were familiar sounds to her ears or where they came from. Did she only hear them in her head? Her heart pounded loudly as she reached the bottom of the stairs.

She saw a small bar and a poker table full of chips, coins, and old faded playing cards but no players. *Where had the sounds come from?* She knew she had heard them loud and clear when walking down the stairs.

A smaller table sat against the rear wall. Next to it Cheryl saw a cellar behind metal bars brown with corrosion. It looked like a mining shaft full of old whiskey barrels, ladders, and such. That vault-shaped cellar looked rather messy, resembling an antique junk yard.

Cheryl turned toward the three wooden doors to her right opposite the gambling area. They were painted in a shabby looking green color. Each one of them was closed and locked, but the museum owners had removed a board in the middle of the first two doors so one could glance into the sparsely lit, small rooms. Cheryl gasped at the sight.

Inside the first room stood a bed, a small, antique armoire, and a nightstand holding a petroleum lamp next to a cheval mirror. The wallpaper sported a faded flower design that most likely had been a rich red during its best days. But now it had turned into stain-battered brown that peeled from the walls in more than one spot. An antique cast iron stove stood in a corner near the mirror. The threadbare mat at the foot of the bed had faded and showed holes.

Cheryl looked into the room and felt a powerful sensation of emotional pain. A small handwritten sign next to the door explained to visitors that this was one of the original prostitution rooms of the higher priced calico queens.

She kept staring into the tiny chamber, imagining how women followed their trade in here while men on the other side of the door gambled at the poker table. Whoever sat there must have been aware of the events taking place on the other side of the wooden wall. Everybody down here would have seen the men entering those rooms with the soiled doves. *Did they pay attention, or were they too hypnotized by the poker cards and the stack of money and silver on the table,* she wondered.

She felt a pang of grief as she imagined the abuse those women must have faced and glanced at the dusty cheval mirror. It had gone half blind with age. Its carved wooden frame holding the glass was a beautiful example of antique craftsmanship.

Cheryl looked into that very mirror through the opening in the door and saw her face reflecting blurrily. But strangely the face did not resemble hers. A dark-haired woman with huge eyes looked back at her, a sad yet knowing smile on her face.

The museum's visitor was too shocked to move. She blinked a couple of times, hoping her eyes only played a trick on her in the semidarkness of the basement. When she opened them again, the woman was still there and raised her hand, motioning Cheryl to come in.

CHAPTER 16

BEING A SHADY LADY

*M*ae knew if she wanted to make good money and continue to work at the Bird Cage Theatre, there was no way out. She had to offer herself to the men who paid for her company. Fortunately, she was considered for the downstairs bordello rooms and not the cheap cribs above the main theatre.

Down here in the basement was where the big money rolled. It was the place where the gents who were better off would seek services of personal pleasures from her. But Mae also knew that those kinds of men had the tendency to ask for more exotic kinds of sexual practices and were way more demanding due to the higher amount of money they paid. She heard that they sometimes even wanted brutal favors.

The poker game was rolling for months now and had never been interrupted. Lizette had told her that it cost well over a thousand dollars to buy yourself into it as a player, not that there was often a chair available.

"A thousand dollars!" Mae couldn't believe it. Lizette nodded her head eagerly.

"Yes, my dear, there's big money in Tombstone, and believe it or not, so far, they have not even found the mother lode of silver. People assume this town to be the center of the biggest silver strike in history. If you handle them men down here smartly, they will pay you a fortune in silver or pure gold." Lizette rolled up one of her stockings and got ready for her trapeze act. "Mae, you can ask for almost every price considering your looks and dance skills, but what's even better is that you do not have to give your favors to every unwashed, smelly prospector that walks into this establishment. You can select your Johns when you're working down here in the basement rooms. Of course, Hutchinson keeps half of the price for the house. But you will still earn more than enough."

But Mae still had her doubts. "It seems that you really enjoy working here, Lizette. To be honest, I am not so convinced that I will ever be able to feel as comfortable as you do when it comes to offering my body to strangers. But at least I am willing to give it a try, and to see such high stakes on the poker table is indeed a tempting sight. However, I have no intention of living the life of a calico queen for too long. Once I make enough money, I will seek a better future for myself."

Lizette and Crazy Anne took the new girl at the Bird Cage under their wings and taught Mae all the tricks. They showed her how to get guests too drunk so they could not perform their male needs anymore and also how the girls stayed sober themselves by hiding bottles of tea the color of whiskey behind the bar. That way they were able to pretend to drink one shot after the other with the guests who paid for whiskey not knowing that the soiled doves drank cheap tea instead. The bartenders worked hand-in-hand with the soiled doves.

Crazy Anne taught Mae how to emphasize the beauty of her face even more. "Use the juice of raspberries to color your cheeks and mouth. That gives you a healthy look and emphasizes the sensual shape of your lips, dear."

"But how do I avoid getting pregnant?" Lizette pulled her aside.

"Always have some water with lots of lemon juice in your wash bowl. It helps to neutralize the men's seed. You must rinse your private parts with it. Some of us insert a coin as deep as possible to protect the entrance to the womb before we sleep with a man," Lizette added and laughed so hard she had tears streaming down her pale face.

"What's so funny about that?" Mae wanted to know.

"We donate those coins to the old town hags for their church because they talk so nastily about us. Little do they know that our donations are earned in sin in more than one way," Lizette explained and wiped away the tears with the corner of her silk scarf.

Mae joined her laughter. "Don't forget to use small pieces of linen dipped in perfume or rose oil to keep the stench of sweat and cigars away from your skin," Crazy Anne adds. "Oh, and there are some herbs we regularly brew tea from. That tea helps to prevent pregnancies as well."

After learning all she needed to know about performing the world's oldest trade, it did not take long before Mae Davenport was a well sought-after lady of the night at the house of ill repute and was indeed able to select her paying customers according to her liking. The men paid in pure silver coins, and the former carnival singer had gathered a small fortune already.

The only thing that bothered her was what Russian Bill might be thinking of her. They had not spoken since their meal at Nellie Cashman's restaurant. They greeted each other from across the room, but that was it. Somehow his opinion of her mattered a great deal, and she was worried that he looked down on her for being a woman of easy morals now. She wouldn't be astonished if he did.

Mae had moved into Lizette and Crazy Anne's house. The three girls shared the costs and made the place a home where they spent their daytime chatting away happily, cooking, and sewing their own wardrobe. A decent, respected seamstress would not have been willing to be at their service at any time, so they had to help themselves.

All the Bird Cage girls were loved by the men in town yet hated by the so-called pure ladies of the community. The town's "decent" women who gossiped so nastily about the sporting girls at the most famous brothel in Tombstone would have been surprised at how often their beloved husbands spent their time in the arms of the fallen angels. Funny enough though, despite all the bashing against the prostitutes, their money was never rejected when donated to the local church or other institutions of the town. Mae had a strong dislike for hypocrites, so she stayed away from the female population of Tombstone unless they were painted cats like her. She often thought that it served the town's women right that their husbands betrayed them and found it as amusing as Lizette that the coins they donated were soiled with pure sin.

A week later Mae decided to wear the new red bustle dress she had sewn with the help of Crazy Anne. Mae looked absolutely gorgeous in the outfit, and the crimson red material hugged her petite figure. When Mae arrived at the Bird Cage looking stunning that evening, Mister Hutchinson pulled her aside as soon as she walked behind the stage.

"I have a special guest for you tonight, Mae. He paid in advance for the whole night. You get a share of forty dollars in silver." The beautiful woman stared at the owner of the most notorious place in the West.

"Forty dollars? You got to be kidding me." That was a small

fortune, and Mae wondered who was willing to pay such an amount and even a bigger share to Hutchinson to spend an entire night with her. She went downstairs and straight to the first crib next to the poker area and waited for her lover of the night behind the closed door. She hoped that the man did not have any brutal preferences when it came to the physical favors he had paid for. A few days ago, one of the girls had been brutally raped, and her face had been cut with a Bowie knife. With her looks destroyed, only making a living in the shabby cribs on Sixth Street was left for the unfortunate girl. The incident shook up all of the girls in the Bird Cage Theatre and reminded Mae to never forget the dangers of her new life. She had followed Nellie Cashman's advice and had bought a small Derringer which was well hidden under her skirt.

Mae closed the door but still heard the poker game going on with its background sounds of hollering and male cursing and the faint laughter of the girl in the room next door.

She poked at the fire burning in the small stove. It had cooled down in the building and she was thankful for the warm glow of the embers although the air in the room smelled of smoke now. Mae hoped that her lover for the night was a man who took decent care of his body. Although she worked as a prostitute now, she hated bad-smelling men and preferred those who visited the bath house regularly. Often the stench of whiskey and beer together with old sweat was overwhelming upstairs, especially the closer one got to the main bar. Thinking of having to sleep with those sweaty miners was still a gut-wrenching thought for Mae, and she tried to avoid them whenever possible. As long as she had Johns who were willing to pay a high price for her, she was safe from having to offer her service in the cheap upstairs cribs.

She lowered the light of the petroleum lamp and watched her own shadow dance across the wall. As Mae studied the wallpaper with its flowery design, she heard the door opening behind her.

A wave of piano music and loud laughter drifted into the room, which indicated that her lover for the night had entered. Mae was about to turn as a whispering voice asked her to remain standing still with her back to him.

He spoke softly, and she could barely understand what he said, but she heard him moving closer. The man softly touched both of her shoulders. Mae felt his chest leaning against her back and was nervous. She wanted to see who he was, but the unknown feller would not allow her to turn. Not yet. He held her tight, and Mae was getting worried. Then he kissed her neck. It was a gentle caress like the light touch of a feather, and she could not help but enjoy it.

His hands moved from her shoulders down, following her spine to her waist where they rested a moment. Slowly, without hurry, he unlaced the top of her dress and the corset underneath. She held her breath as he slid it from her slender torso.

Mae had never been undressed with such tenderness. His hands traced every inch of her bare skin, and it left her shivering with arousal. It confused her because so far, she had never felt sexual lust when sleeping with a man.

She heard a pocket watch being laid onto the small nightstand and the sound of fabric falling on the floor.

The next thing she felt was a bare, warm chest being pressed against her back while he cradled her into his embrace. He was not in a hurry. They stood skin to skin, soaking up each other's warmth. His chest felt muscular, his stomach flat. The musky scent of his naked torso added to her excitement.

Finally, he spoke to her. "Turn around, Mae," he instructed.

Surprised, the dark-haired woman stared wide-eyed into the handsome features of Russian Bill, and she immediately felt like covering herself, but he shook his head. "Don't feel ashamed, Mae."

"How am I supposed to feel? You paid, so go ahead and take what the price is for." She did not mean to hurt him but was too shocked to learn that he was the one who had paid for a full night with her. Of all the men in this house of sin, Mae Davenport had never wanted him to buy her body. She was behaving ridiculously and knew it, as she was nothing but a servant of sin but could not help her hostile reaction. Shame and grief flushed through her, causing her eyes to burn with tears.

He looked hurt as he pulled back from her and picked up his shirt and vest. "You can keep the money. I do not need to force myself onto a woman, Mae Davenport. Generally, they are far more welcoming than you are," he added with a bitter tone and pressed his lips together in a tight line.

She felt as if he had slapped her across the face. Russian Bill was getting dressed and was about to walk out the door, barely able to control his anger and disappointment. Grabbing the doorknob, he stood still when she called him back.

"Of all the men in this place, you are the only one I am worried about what you may think of me. Who can respect a woman like me? You know how I earn my money, especially now since I work in this place without the carnival group. Why pay that high price, why book me for the entire night? Is your hunger for a woman so endless? Why didn't you pay for a more experienced soiled dove?"

She shivered and held onto her dress. But strangely she did not want him to leave.

Mae was deeply confused, not knowing how to handle these unknown emotions crashing over her like a cold wave. She felt like a fool and ashamed to the bone.

He turned slowly. "I did it because I wanted to be with you the whole night. You, and not just any woman, Mae. I bought your services the entire night because I can't stand the thought of someone else laying hands on you after I share this bed with you. The reason why I paid is because I could not hold back my passion and desire for you any longer, but I was obviously wrong because I thought you felt the same way."

"I do, Bill, but as a woman and not as a soiled dove. I want the same but not for the silver, rather for the sake of feeling you and to touch your heart and soul as much as that body of yours. Yes, I desire you, but you see me as the sporting woman I am because you paid to lay hands on me and never showed that you felt anything for me as a man at all."

She spun, feeling devastated. *This is all wrong. He should not be here. I should not be here,* Mae thought. Her eyes were moist with tears. She could not hold back any longer. He looked back at her and walked over to where she stood like an insecure child with tears streaming down her flushed cheeks. Bill seemed drawn to her like a moth to a flame. As he raised her chin with his fingers, he forced her to look into his eyes that had turned smoky dark gray with desire. Russian Bill was glaring down at her, a demanding expression on his face.

"Then prove to me that you want me, Mae. Let me feel it."

He didn't wait for her to answer but kissed her, hard and passionately, and Mae returned that kiss with a hunger previously unknown to her. Mae had tried to imagine what it would be like to kiss him, but nothing prepared her for the intense feeling that raged through her body like a flame. She was swept away by the sensuality of his kiss and the way her body reacted to his.

The Bird Cage Theatre and the poker game outside vanished in a storm of passion and lust that raged behind the door of the first chamber. Neither held anything back. Mae and Russian Bill didn't only surrender to their desire for each other, but also to the feelings which had grown constantly and were not controllable any longer. The two lovers conquered each other's body, explored every inch of skin, and bathed in each other's passion for hours. Every touch of him gave Mae the feeling of being complete, as if she found a long missing part of herself in his arms.

"When I look into your eyes, I can see my own soul," she whispered. He held her tight, and when they united their bodies, it felt to them as if their hearts melted together, beating at the same unique rhythm one feels only once in a lifetime.

They drowned in each other's lust, not willing to give in to physical exhaustion. The night was still young, and Russian Bill bought Mae until dawn with the shine of the silver dollars he had placed in Hutchinson's hands. He would make her his for that night and hopefully for good.

"You are my future, Mae, for now and for eternity. I shall never let you go, my love."

CHAPTER 17

THE SMELL OF DEATH

*C*heryl stared back at the image in the dusty mirror. A light flavor of cherry cigars hung in the air. She touched her lips. *Have I felt those kisses? It seemed so real.*

There was a whispering voice all around her, yet it seemed to echo in her head. "Do you still feel me, Mae? I missed you for such a long time."

As Cheryl turned around to follow the sound of the voice, she looked back at the small cellar at the end of the narrow corridor that led along the cribs. It was blocked by an iron gate and looked as if it extended all the way under the stage above. The dirt floor was covered with an array of old artifacts such as wine barrels, glass bottles, even an old school bench, and much more. Everything seemed tossed into the vault cellar without a plan, as if remaining items of the Bird Cage's yesteryear days had been thrown in there in a hurry.

The door of the third chamber was closed. No board had been removed. It was not possible to glance into that room. Nevertheless, Cheryl walked toward it. A small sign announced that this chamber would be opening soon for public viewing.

According to the given information, this had been the bathroom and changing room for the gamblers who spent countless hours at the poker table.

Cheryl's steps brought her closer, and she reluctantly touched the locked door. Although made of wood, it felt unusually cold, and the moment her fingertips touched the door's surface, she was overwhelmed with the sudden stench of decaying flesh seeping through the wood. She stumbled backward, retching, and bumped against the banister in front of the gambling area.

"Mae, stay away from that room! I cannot protect you if you enter there," the voice echoed in her head, an urgent sounding whisper with a threatening tone.

Cheryl quickly walked away from the vault cellar and the locked door and stumbled into the next room of the museum. Although the stench nearly made her gag, she still felt as if she should stay close to the cribs. The farther her feet led her from the basement chambers, the sadder she felt. For some reason she did not want to leave but couldn't explain the confusing longing.

The adjoining room displayed many old photos and documents such as prostitute licenses that permitted the ladies of the line to offer their services in the world's oldest trade. To her surprise there was even one framed at the rear wall for Mae Davenport.

A single tear rolled over Cheryl's cheek. She knew she was somehow connected to the destiny of Mae but did not understand how and why. To read her name on the framed paper yellowed with age made the weird visions that bothered Cheryl even more realistic.

"Good heavens, what in the world was that terrible smell?" she mumbled, still feeling nauseated. Cheryl walked back to the main entrance. The lady there smiled at her.

"Did you enjoy your tour? Any questions?"

"Have you ever heard of a woman called Mae Davenport?" Cheryl asked.

"Hmmm, let me think. Oh, yes, now I remember. She came to Tombstone during its silver boom heydays, like most of the girls, of course. Mae was a member of a carnival group but stayed behind when the troop left for another boomtown if I recall correctly. She continued to work as a soiled dove or prostitute, as you would call them today. We display her license issued by the town's marshal of that time. And guess what, it was indeed the famous Virgil Earp who signed that very document. The town made lots of money with the women of loose morals. Each lady of the night had to pay a fee to the city or she wouldn't have been allowed to offer her services. The town council had them examined by the doctor at least once a month to avoid spreading disease. Much smarter than nowadays if you ask me."

Cheryl was fascinated. "So, the townsfolk treated the calico queens like outcasts but accepted their money nevertheless, although it was earned in sin."

The museum employee nodded eagerly. "Yes, indeed, that's the way it was. By the way, I'm Teresa. I'm sorry I was so busy opening this place up this morning, and I didn't even introduce myself."

The student took her outstretched hand. "Cheryl. Pleasure to meet you, Teresa."

The lady behind the old bar looked thoughtful for a moment. "You know, not all folks in town disliked the shady ladies. The men, the miners, of course loved them. It was hard work to dig for silver and many died much too young. Some drowned in the flooded mines because the deeper they dug, the higher the ground-water level rose. Some lost their lives in collapsing shafts, and many of them passed away because of consumption —tuberculosis—like our famous Doc Holliday. A lot of prospectors got killed by syphilis and gave that disease to many working girls as well. All these men were so thankful for the female attention they got, so they didn't mind having to pay for it. In my opinion the fallen angels indeed built up the frontier and conquered the West at least as much as all the miners, cowboys, and gunfighters did, if not more."

"Sounds as if you are actually very fond of them, Teresa." Cheryl looked at the older woman who was dressed in a romantic mint green Victorian bustle dress adorned with black lace. She wore a matching hat with small black feathers attached to it on a silver-colored hatband. Teresa looked so authentic she could have stepped right out of an 1882 Western scene.

The friendly woman patted Cheryl's hand. "You've only been here a few weeks. You'll understand much more about their life soon, believe me. I admit, you're right, I am very fond of the ladies of the night. I studied a lot about them. So did your boss, Dorothea, by the way. Some of the women were tragic personalities. A considerable number of them were so unhappy they committed suicide. Many were alcoholics and laudanum addicts, but believe me, if their help was needed, they always stood by the needy ones. Some of the madams running brothels opened their places during times of disease and took care of the sick. They converted their houses of ill fame into hospitals and pampered many sick miners back to life without charging them."

Teresa laughed at Cheryl's surprised facial expression. "Not the kind of behavior one would expect when talking of prostitutes, right? But it's the truth. The Courthouse Museum even has historical paperwork proving it. Ask Dorothea, she might be able to show you some of the documents."

Cheryl nodded. Then she shook Teresa's hand again. "Thank you for your patience and explanations, Teresa. I hope to chat with you another time. But there's a group of tourists walking over, so I don't want to keep you from work any longer."

"You're always welcome, sweetie. Visit me again. Check my working hours with Heather. It's great to meet someone who's genuinely interested in the history here."

Cheryl was about to walk out the door but suddenly recalled that she wanted to tell the museum employee one more thing, so she turned around. "Teresa, I almost forgot! Down there in the area of the third door opposite the small bar, it smells really bad like a dead animal rotting away or something."

The lady behind the counter hesitated. "Must be a critter or a stray cat. Most likely it snuck in during the day and couldn't find a way out. Happens from time to time. Well, it won't smell for long. Everything is so dry here, it'll mummify pretty fast."

Cheryl doubted that explanation. "If it's in the third room, I think it would be easier to remove it before the smell gets too bad. Well, thinking of it, it is gut wrenching already."

But the museum employee shook her head looking worried, and Cheryl saw the fear flickering in her eyes. "Girl, none of us ever enters the third room. It's not safe." She quickly turned away and pretended to count her change while she waited for the tourists who were slowly strolling toward the door, debating whether they should spend the money on the admission fee or not.

There was no chance to ask Teresa what she had meant about the room not being safe as the eager employee had already started greeting the tourists. Cheryl could not shake off the feeling that Teresa was relieved that she didn't have to answer the question.

The young woman turned and left and missed the worried expression on Teresa's face.

On the way back to her temporary home, Cheryl bought two books at a local bookstore—*Soiled Doves of the West* and *Tombstone's Red-Light District*. She planned to spend the rest of the day reading and enjoying her time off.

As soon as she arrived home, Cheryl started her beloved coffee maker and prepared herself some pasta. Not the typical Western cuisine for her, but spaghetti with meat sauce was her personal soul food, and she enjoyed cooking it, especially when she was off.

Soon the house was filled with mouthwatering aromas, and Cheryl fixed herself a plate of the tasty Italian meal. She always took pride in her talents as a cook even if she ate alone. While eating at the kitchen table, her thoughts returned to the historical theatre and to the face she had seen in that cheval mirror of the downstairs crib. *Did that really happen, or is my imagination going wild with all this weird stuff?*

Her modern education forbade her to believe any of this was real, but somehow in a corner of her mind she knew there was more to it.

The voice she'd been hearing on and off sounded so familiar and comforting, as if she had heard it a thousand times, but where? The smell of the cherry cigars was a pleasant flavor, although she didn't smoke at all and had never cared for the aroma.

When she finished her meal, she poured herself some coffee, sat on the porch, and opened the first book, *Red-Light District of Tombstone* by Ben Traywick. According to the information at the back of the book, he was an historian and lived in Tombstone. The picture suggested that he was quite an old man, and Cheryl wondered if he was still alive, as the book had been published years ago.

She read the first few lines and was hooked by the first chapter and picture right away. Her coffee sat on the small table next to her rocking chair, forgotten, like the traffic moving up and down the street from time to time.

She barely looked up when a car or motorcycle drove by and

even forgot to wave at the stagecoach team rattling along the street on their way home.

Her reading was only interrupted once for a necessary stop at the bathroom and to grab her warm shawl. With one foot folded under her lap, the student continued reading. The book was about the hardships and the money made in the red-light district, which originally covered an unbelievable six blocks of old Tombstone. Cheryl looked at the pictures of the women printed in the paperback book and touched their cheeks gently. Some of them got introduced with their own chapter or even a few pages, and Cheryl assumed that these were the more famous women among the soiled doves of Tombstone's rowdy past.

When she flipped a page, a young woman's face stared back at her from a haunting, sepia-colored image. The soiled dove looked fragile yet gorgeous with long wavy hair which appeared to be a fiery copper tone in the portrait.

Cheryl stared at the picture. She was not even aware of her own tears. The only emotion she felt was the shock of recognition before she read the text at the bottom. Lizette. *I recognize her, but how is that possible?* The fallen angel had lived over a hundred years ago, yet Cheryl knew her. She sobbed as she read about Lizette's success as the "Flying Nymph" at the Bird Cage Theatre. She performed swinging back and forth across the entire theatre room on a trapeze with daring costumes of half transparent fabric. She must have been quite a sight, and Cheryl imagined her flying through the air like a gorgeous butterfly. As she read the chapter about Lizette on the next page, she learned about her unstable mentality and how she lived through years of self-destruction caused by a life filled with alcohol and laudanum abuse. Lizette had ended her existence on her own terms by committing suicide.

"Oh, girl, why in the world?" Cheryl whispered, feeling devastated as if she had lost a close friend.

When Cheryl stopped reading, she had reached the last page of the book, and it was getting dark. *Oh, my goodness, it is evening already. I didn't feel the time passing by.* Cheryl had been so captivated by the paperback she hadn't realized that the sun set behind the Courthouse Museum.

She turned the pages back to the pictures of Mae Davenport and of Lizette, whose family name remained a secret hidden in the past.

Cheryl's Tombstone adventure felt like an unusual dream, and for the first time in her life, the modern days with its cars, mobile phones, and computers appeared unreal and strange to her.

She slowly walked into the house and stared at the TV in the tiny living room. It sat there on the sideboard like an unwanted intruder on top of the beautifully crafted furniture. The electronic device didn't fit in at all. It stood for a different time and a different world. She didn't bother to turn it on but instead showered and went straight to bed, for the first time in months switching her phone off. She felt exhausted.

Her dreams were filled with images of a crowded saloon and a beautiful Lizette swinging above the audience on a thin cable made of steel. The "Flying Nymph" smiled at Cheryl in her dreams, and Cheryl smiled back at the soiled dove.

CHAPTER 18

THE EVIL SIDE OF THE BIRD CAGE THEATRE

The next day Dorothea invited Cheryl to have dinner with her right after work. The young woman asked her boss about Mae Davenport, and the manager of the courthouse shared what she knew.

"Mae came to town with a carnival group, but when the artists left, she stayed in Tombstone as a woman of ill fame. She probably made much more money in that trade. Rumor had it that she was seriously involved with a gambler by the name of Russian Bill who was a regular at the Bird Cage Theatre. He was another tragic figure of the silver boom and claimed to be the son of a noblewoman in Russia. That's how he got his nickname. Fact is, he died under tragic circumstances. Wanted so much to be an outlaw, and in the end, I think he was sentenced to death over a crime he didn't even commit. Mae was said to have been madly in love with him and never got over losing the love of her life. Something tragic must have happened, but so far, we have not found any further traces of their lives and where she went after Tombstone."

The waitress of The Depot restaurant brought their pizza. As they started to eat, Cheryl asked her friend where she had gotten all the information. Dorothea hesitated for a moment. When she spoke, her cheeks blushed. "Most of it from doing research in old town papers. When we took over the Courthouse Museum, we found a whole bunch of old documents stored in boxes in the attic. But Crazy Anne told me quite a few tales as well."

"Who was Crazy Anne again?" Cheryl waited for the answer and stopped chewing for a moment. Dorothea shrugged her shoulders.

"As a matter of fact, Crazy Anne is my great-grandmother, the one who owned the house you're staying in."

Cheryl still didn't get it. "So, you must have found a diary or something like that. How awesome."

But the woman sitting across from her shook her head. "No, Cheryl, she speaks to me about these things."

Cheryl stared and didn't know what to say. An embarrassing silence spread between them. Dorothea raised her hands as if to apologize.

"I know this is hard to believe, and I don't expect you to. You asked me a straightforward question, and I answered it honestly. I have seen Crazy Anne numerous times, and, believe me, at the beginning I doubted my own sanity. When I saw her the first time, I bought a new pair of glasses thinking maybe there was something wrong with my eyes. After a few appearances she started to talk to me. Each time I heard her voice loud and clear. Crazy Anne told me things about the old days in Tombstone, which were confirmed in some of the documents I mentioned to you. The people she named, the trials that took place, it's all there in those records. Prostitutes and performers of the Bird Cage she told me about, they all really existed. There were details you can't find in the tourist books or souvenir shops.

Believe me, it scared the wits out of me in the beginning. When I told Bert about it, he was about to sign me up for a loony bin. But then, one day he saw her, too. That was when we got knee-deep into research, wanting to find out the truth. Everything she told me proved to be true."

Cheryl shook her head. She liked the McEntires a lot, and somehow she knew the woman was not making up the story. Yet she could not bring herself to believe all this. She had been brought up in the world of science and modern education.

This whole town seemed stuck in the 1880s in more ways than one. And apparently Tombstone changed the people living here. *Who in the world believes in spirits of yesteryear roaming the streets of an old Western town,* Cheryl wondered and swallowed a bite of her pizza, but she wasn't hungry anymore.

The rest of the evening passed with shallow small talk. Somehow the normally so enjoyable conversation between the two women suffered after talking about the strange topic, and both women were glad when the waitress came with their check to end the dinner invitation. After paying and putting on their jackets, they walked to Dorothea's truck, but Cheryl told her she would rather walk home. Dorothea hesitated a moment but then wished her a good night.

"Okay, Cheryl, see you tomorrow at the Courthouse. Thanks for joining me for dinner. Have a great night, my friend." Then Dorothea got into her truck and backed out of the parking lot.

The California student waved goodbye and watched the pickup's rear lights disappear around the corner. She walked slowly along the quiet street, lost in thought about what her friend had told her about Crazy Anne.

A sudden cold breeze across her cheeks made her raise her gaze, wondering where the chilly wind came from as it had been a mild evening when she left the restaurant. She hadn't paid attention to where she was and now realized that she stood in front of the Bird Cage Theatre.

The old structure sure looked different at night. She felt a tugging sensation toward the building, and goosebumps started to show on her arms. If she hadn't known better, she would have said the building was calling her, wanting to lure her to come inside. That was when Cheryl heard a menacing voice that came from nowhere and called her.

"You're supposed to get to work. Come on over here. You're late." The voice wasn't the one she had heard before. It was more like a growl. She walked toward the main entrance with its brown double doors, not aware of where her steps took her.

"Do not make me come for you. Get to work right now!" The cold breeze was all around Cheryl now like an icy storm, and for some reason she feared the source of the voice. Her heart felt as if squeezed in a deadly grip, and her own pulse echoed in her ears as she was about to touch the front door, although her gut feeling told her to run away. She panicked when she found that her legs would not obey the order of her brain to turn away from the building. But then the sudden aroma of the cherry cigar smoke enfolded her.

"Mae, my love, you must leave now. He is evil and will not let you go if you step through the entrance now." The pleasant voice she knew so well was an urgent whisper close to her right ear.

She felt someone standing next to her but couldn't see a soul on the street. But she somehow knew she could trust the voice and finally managed to turn around and followed the aroma of the cigar smoke that led her farther down Allen Street and away from the old museum. All she knew was that whoever led her away from the Bird Cage would not harm her. Cheryl walked as if in a trance, and suddenly she stood in front of her guest house.

"Mae, you can never enter the Bird Cage at night unless you are with me."

Cheryl shook her head. "My name is Cheryl. I don't know who you are and why, for Christ's sake, you don't show yourself to me, you coward!"

There was a moment of silence, and she turned to unlock her door. "That may be your name now, but your real name is Mae, Mae Davenport." As the words vanished into the night, Cheryl stared into the darkness. The smell of the cigars was gone.

The perplexed woman was frustrated and bothered by the outcome of the evening. What had happened in front of that old brothel? The man who had called her for work sounded rude, furious, and somehow dangerous. And then there was that second voice which she had heard a couple of times before. So kind and soothing. Its sound tugged at some part of her subconscious. *I know that voice from somewhere, but every time I think I remember it slips my mind again. I seem to know that man, but I cannot make a connection. Who is he?*

Cheryl was also deeply disturbed by the way the evening with Dorothea had gone at the restaurant and was afraid she might have been unkind to her superior, whom she considered to be a dear friend by now. What if she hurt Dorothea's feelings by not taking her story serious. "I have to apologize tomorrow," Cheryl said into the empty room. *After all, who am I to judge other people's beliefs?*

She went to bed still upset and tossed and turned into the throes of a nightmare where she was in a room filled with thick smoke. The stage was filled with can-can dancers, and the men were on their feet clapping and cheering. But Cheryl was on the way to the basement where she knew the stranger who spoke so tenderly to her would be waiting. In her dream she walked downstairs to the first crib with its green wooden door. She opened it, stepped through it, and saw him turn and smile at her. She recognized his face in her dream. His wavy, long hair framed his handsome features. His gray-blue eyes looked at her with a warmth that sent shivers down her spine, and his sensual lips were curled into a welcoming smile as he held out a hand. She rushed into his arms and whispered, "Bill, my beloved Russian Bill."

CHAPTER 19

SPEAKING WITH THE SPIRITS

*C*heryl woke with a splitting headache. She brewed her coffee stronger than usual and swallowed two aspirins, hoping they would work quickly. Tired, she closed her bloodshot eyes and rubbed her temples. Immediately, Cheryl saw the face from her dreams before her inner eye and felt a warm tingle in her belly.

My God, get yourself together, woman. It's ridiculous that you're dreaming of an outlaw from the 1880s and having the hots for him. Good gracious, you must miss civilization too much. But however much she scolded herself, the events and dreams of the last evening didn't vanish and to her annoyance even caused her to smile.

When she met Dorothea at work, she had made up her mind to talk openly about last evening's topic with her. Dorothea greeted her warmly but hesitated to start a conversation. But before Cheryl could talk to her, the sheriff walked into the museum, greeting them with a tip to his cowboy hat.

"Good morning, ladies. I am here to inform you that we have

called off the search for Lisa. It looks like she ran away from town. And even if she didn't, this is going to be a cold case nevertheless, until new evidence pops up. Just wanted to let you know. But remember, if you come across anything connected to this case, I surely would appreciate it if you called me." After giving the information, he left the two women standing in the entrance hall of the Courthouse Museum.

"Such a shame. Just like it had been with the other women. Not finding any evidence so they give up. It's always the same with the authorities here," Dorothea added with a sad smile.

"Why don't we ask Crazy Anne? She might know something about it." Her elder friend turned around likely thinking it was a sarcastic remark from Cheryl, but when she saw the young woman's face, it didn't show sarcasm but rather worry.

"So, you believe me?"

Cheryl nodded. Only then Dorothea realized how pale her trainee was under her makeup that morning.

"What happened to make you change your mind?"

"I don't see them. But I hear something all the time, and yesterday when I walked by that old theatre...."

Her elder friend looked at her, shocked. "The Bird Cage? It calls you, doesn't it?" Cheryl simply nodded.

"Listen, darling, we have to take care of today's business now, but we'll talk tonight. I'll come to your place if that's okay. You can tell me exactly what happened last night. Don't forget, it was Crazy Anne's home, and she might have a thing or two to say about all this. There is nothing you have to be scared of, except maybe nighttime. This town lives a different life once the sun sets."

The day seemed to drag on endlessly, and Cheryl was glad when it was time to lock up at the museum.

When she checked her watch, she still had enough time to

shower and prepare a light meal at her antique home. Dorothea arrived right on time at 7:30, but Cheryl barely recognized her at first.

The lady wore an 1880s-style dress with a bustle made from beautifully embroidered plaid material. A gorgeous hat in matching colors covered most of Dorothea's hair. The big paper bag she carried seemed even odder than her unusual wardrobe.

"What in the world?" Cheryl wondered, but her visitor hushed her with an index finger on her lips.

"I brought this bustle dress for you. It should fit. Please try it on."

Cheryl laughed. "Are we going to a costume contest or a saloon or what?"

Her friend was not surprised by the other woman's reaction. "Cheryl, in order to understand the old days and the people who lived here, you should feel like one of them. Communication with spirits from the past comes so much easier then. Wearing these clothes might help."

"You've got to be kidding me, Dorothea."

"Give it a try. You have nothing to lose, do you?" Dorothea pulled a beautiful, shiny dress in a rich green color out of the bag. Cheryl didn't want to offend her friend again and reluctantly agreed. She took the dress into the bedroom to change. At first, she did not know how to put it on, but then she managed, and surprisingly, the skirt and the lace embroidered jacket fit perfectly.

When Cheryl turned and looked at the old-fashioned dressing mirror that resembled the one in the downstairs room at the Bird Cage Theatre, she gasped in disbelief. The reflection in the mirror didn't look like her. She stared into the face of a stranger. A step toward the door caused the silky material to produce a rustling sound. The clothes felt unexpectedly comfortable, and the sound of the material was somewhat familiar.

Cheryl walked into the living room where Dorothea waited, sitting on the antique sofa with a thoughtful expression on her face. "Oh my God, look at you! How beautiful, Cheryl! This outfit is made for you, the color, the fit, simply everything. Good heavens, you look as if you stepped out of the 1880s into this very room."

At first, it was kind of weird for Cheryl to sit and eat in another woman's clothes, but to her surprise she started to feel different wearing them. Even her language changed— Cheryl avoided modern words without being aware of it. She thought about taking a photo of her wearing this precious outfit, but for the first time in many months, she could not remember where she had left her cell phone. It simply didn't matter.

When the plates were cleared and a pot of fresh coffee set on the table, Dorothea suggested lighting the two antique oil lamps.

"Isn't it dangerous to use them in an old house?" Cheryl wondered.

"No, they work well. I use them quite often, and, to be frank, Crazy Anne cannot stand modern electricity."

Cheryl didn't dare question that remark and followed Dorothea's advice. The living room grew darker, but the light of the flickering flame spread a warm glow. After a few moments both flames stabilized, and they adjusted the wick slightly. The oil in the lamps spread a pleasant smell of roses.

"Whatever happens now, try to remain open-minded," Dorothea said. Cheryl sat nervously on the antic sofa.

Dorothea looked around the room and remained silent for a few moments. When she spoke, it made Cheryl jump.

"Crazy Anne, I am sure you have seen my friend Cheryl around in this beautiful house of yours. She loves your home,

Anne. My friend here helps me at the museum and is in town to learn the history. You can tell us so much about the old days in Tombstone. Cheryl is bothered by things she hears when she walks around town at night. She sees things in her dreams. Can you explain to us why all this is happening to her?"

The room remained silent. Cheryl didn't know what to expect. When the silence stretched out for several minutes she was about to get up and ask herself what she was doing here dressed as if she had stepped out of a Hollywood studio prop room. Was she actually trying to talk to the ghost of a woman who died in the early 1900s? This was simply ridiculous.

Just when she was about to get up from her chair and call the whole thing off, she heard a soft female whisper. Or did Cheryl's ears fool her again? There! There it was again. Loud and clear.

"The Bird Cage."

Dorothea looked at Cheryl who stared back at her, her face a mask of disbelief.

Dorothea asked into the gloomy living room. "The Bird Cage? What's wrong with it?"

"He is calling her to come back to him," the voice whispered.

"Who wants her back? Is Cheryl called to come to the theatre? Why?"

No answer. Cheryl shook her head. Just as both women thought the conversation was over, the whispering voice came again.

"Russian Bill—he wants Mae to come back. He still loves and needs her. He has been waiting for her all these years. But beware, Hutchinson will not let her go. The greedy pimp needs women for the brothel. He did not want to let her leave in the old days, and he will not let her go now if she returns there."

"But, Crazy Anne, what does Cheryl have to do with all this?" Dorothea asked into the dark corner from where the voice seemed to come. But there was no answer anymore. Whoever had been whispering to them was gone like a gentle breeze at dawn.

Dorothea stared at Cheryl who had gone pale. "What in the world is happening here? Who has been talking to us?" Cheryl wanted to know. Dorothea got up and turned on the lights.

Cheryl closed her eyes. The sudden glare of the ceiling fixture blinded her a moment, and she missed the calm, yellowish light of the oil lamps.

The rustle of Dorothea's dress was a comforting sound, but Cheryl's heart pounded in her chest as if she had run up and down Allen Street. She couldn't help but rub her arms to chase away the goosebumps.

"What does all this mean? Was she talking about Mae Davenport?"

Her friend sat silently for a moment, sipping on her coffee that had grown cold in its delicate porcelain cup. Cheryl offered to brew a fresh one, but Dorothea shook her head at the offer.

"It looks like you have some sort of connection to that historical building or its spirits. It almost sounded as if you have something to do with Mae Davenport," Dorothea mused, but the younger woman shook her head.

"I heard the name for the first time a couple of days ago when I read it on a city license at the museum and then again in a book about the former red-light district in this town."

"I know it sounds weird, but there has to be some sort of link," Dorothea said.

"Who is that Hutchinson guy the voice spoke about?" Cheryl wondered. The name somehow worried her and gave her the chills. It rang a bell, but she could not recall where she had stumbled across the name before.

"He was the owner of the place during its early days," Dorothea explained. "Hutchinson used to work in a theatre before, so he and his wife originally planned to provide theatre entertainment for the whole family, but no respectable woman of Tombstone ever set foot in his premises. So, the soiled doves took over the place as their favorite playground within a few weeks only. The owner understood pretty fast that if he allowed the women of easy morals to roam the Bird Cage, the men would flock into the theatre in higher numbers and most likely spend a lot of money on them girls and drinks. Definitely more cash than the respectable married women would, not that they ever considered to be seen in the place to start with."

"Sounds like Hutchinson was a real crook taking advantage of the girls," Cheryl remarked.

"You got that right. The crowd that lingered in the Bird Cage played right into Hutchinson's pockets, and it did not take longer than a month, and he and his wife turned the place into a brothel, saloon, and gambling hall forgetting about morals standards for the sake of the money earned.

"It's said that he got greedy and started to abuse the ladies of the night and would rarely let the very successful ones leave the place again. The sad thing is that many of them died of disease or alcohol abuse. Quite a high number of the soiled doves even committed suicide. Very few of those calico queens got lucky and found a reasonable man to marry. Hutchinson most likely didn't fancy that, as it meant losing a good pony in his stable, so to speak. I can imagine he must have acted like a dangerous, controlling pimp. After all, there was a lot of money in prostitution."

Cheryl remained silent. Something about this explanation sounded familiar, but she couldn't put it into words. The thoughts were stuck as if in thick fog, and she couldn't quite get hold of them. The feeling vanished as fast as it had appeared.

"Well, it's getting late for an old lady like me." Dorothea stifled a yawn.

Cheryl asked her to wait a moment so she could change her clothes and return the dress, but her friend shook her head.

"I don't fit into that outfit anymore. You may keep it as a souvenir to remind you of your time in Tombstone whenever you get ready to leave for California again."

Cheryl touched the skirt gently. "This is an expensive material not even mentioning the hours of sewing that went into it. How can I accept such a gift?"

"The color and size fit you much better than it ever fit me. Go on and keep it." Cheryl embraced the elderly woman, deeply touched by her generosity.

She waved goodbye and watched Dorothea drive off toward the Courthouse, but she remained standing on the porch leaning against one of the white posts, staring into the darkness. She was lost in thought when a male voice next to her side made her jump.

"You look so lovely tonight, Mae. I've always loved that color on you." It was the gentle, husky voice she knew well by now. A pleasant tingle moved from her stomach to her chest.

She blushed slightly. The scent of a cherry cigar tickled her nostrils. Finally, after countless days of just hearing his voice and smelling the tobacco, she saw the shadow of a tall man leaning against the pole of the porch. His hair fell thick and wavy onto his broad shoulders, yet it wasn't moved by the gentle evening breeze. His eyes were hidden in the shadows.

Cheryl should have been scared to death. But to her astonishment she was not, despite the fact that she could see the Courthouse Museum's brick wall down the road shimmering through the handsome figure standing beside her. His face was rather blurry, but nevertheless, she knew it was him and would have recognized him anywhere as the man she had seen during her vision in front of the poker booth.

The silky skirt softly rustled against her legs as she slowly moved toward him. He held his arms wide open for her, and as he pulled her next to his muscular chest, she could finally feel his solid flesh.

The houses on the other side of the street and parked cars vanished, and the scenery changed drastically. The woman in the green dress found herself standing on the dusty street in the middle of Tombstone's silver boom heydays.

CHAPTER 20

THE PLOT OF THE ENEMY

*E*mbracing each other in front of Crazy Anne's house, the two lovers did not hide how deeply they felt for each other.

Crazy Anne waved at the two love birds. She was happy for Mae Davenport. Russian Bill was a good man to have, and it seemed that he finally found his future in the loving arms of Mae. None of the three paid attentions to Hutchinson, the owner of the Bird Cage, who stood across the road.

His face bore a hateful mask of anger. The people in town were aware that Hutchinson had changed lately. He had made a fortune by allowing the fallen angels to ply their trade at his premises, and by now the theatre attracted famous performers from all over the country who wanted to sing and dance on the famous Bird Cage stage. The nightly crowd got entertained with theatre plays and the daring French Can-can dances, singers, and musicians. The success of the establishment had turned Hutchinson into a greedy individual without scruples.

The brothel had a never-ending demand for fresh women. After all, it was the sporting girls that guaranteed the miners would spend their hard-earned silver at the gambling tables and in the sparsely furnished cribs above the stage or down in the basement rooms. The owner was not a fool. Like every brothel owner along the frontier, he knew that any serious romance developing between a guest and one of his soiled doves would eventually lead to losing the girl as a source of steady income. "I have to end this love affair between Russian Bill and Mae Davenport as fast as possible," he whispered and spit onto the ground while he stared over at the couple which still embraced each other happily. Mae had become a real magnet to the crowd, especially now that Lizette had developed into an unpredictable drunk with suicidal tendencies. Lizette's laudanum and alcohol abuse had started to show, and her beauty was fading. At least he and some of his most reliable guests claimed so. One never knew what that crazy ginger head would do next. She had a short fuse temper, and Hutchinson saw that she hurt herself on purpose during one of her laudanum spells. "I have to replace that nutty redhead witch before she harms anybody else. The hell I will do watching calmly how one of my best ponies might walk out of the Bird Cage for good in addition to this lunatic and her crazy trapeze act."

No, Hutchinson was not willing to lose Mae to her Prince Charming. And neither did he want to give up on that Tattenbaum fellow as a regular guest. He walked along the street, grumbling while looking for a cigar in his vest pocket. "Who the hell knows? Mae might even talk Russian Bill into giving up his gambling habit. I cannot let that happen. That European fool pays me a fortune for his poker booth every night."

The owner of the notorious honky-tonk stomped across the dusty street toward one of the town's shabbier saloons while a devious strategy developed in his evil mind. By the time he entered the tent saloon with its stale odor of old beer and cigar smoke, he had laid out the perfect plan of how to end the liaison between the two lovers.

He would have to sacrifice some income for a short while, but if it worked out the way he planned, he would be the winner in the end. His plan would keep both of them linked to his theatre. All he had to achieve was to make sure that Mae stopped loving Russian Bill.

The table at the rear end of the tent was occupied with some mean-looking, unshaved owl hoots who concentrated on their poker game while sharing a bottle of the cheapest, watered-down whiskey available in town.

Hutchinson walked over to the saddle tramps and greeted them, but they didn't bother looking up. He pulled a chair to the table and waved at the bartender as he pointed to a bottle of the higher-quality corn juice on the top rack of the crude bar. The owner of the Bird Cage motioned the barkeep to bring the bottle to their table. Knowing that Hutchinson could afford to buy the booze he nodded and swiftly hurried to the table with the whiskey.

"A hard-working gentleman deserves a better drink and the company of some beautiful women, don't you think?" Just as expected, he got their attention right away. All three dropped their cards face-down and stared, waiting for him to spill the beans and tell them what he wanted. Everybody in town was aware that these were true scalawags with nothing much to lose. The procurer, on the other hand, took a high risk to mingle with such low lives, so he played it very carefully with them.

"Gentleman, I can offer you an unforgettable week with the most beautiful women of the trade and some money to enjoy some fine whiskey and cigars if you help me get rid of a minor problem."

One of the road agents looked around and pointed at his

companions. "This is Jeff, my brother Pete, and I'm Four Finger Jack, for obvious reason,"

Holding up his left hand, Hutchinson saw that the man's ring finger was missing. As he stared at the man's hand and the small stump, Four Finger Jack explained, "I held a wrong card in my left hand, and the fellow I played poker with shot off my finger over it."

"Now why would a card be wrong that calls for having your hand injured like that?"

"Happened to be the Queen of Hearts, and unfortunately, that card was lying on the table already. Tried to push my luck a bit with a second deck of cards in my vest pocket. But as you see, I managed to escape, thanks to my brother Pete."

The bartender set a bottle of the better corn juice on the table, and the three men helped themselves to a generous shot, throwing the lousier quality in their glasses against the canvas wall of the tent. Hutchinson refused the offered glass as he needed to keep his mind clear.

"Okay, Bird Cage pimp, what is it you need from us?"

The sophisticated man squirmed at the name he was called and looked back at the bartender who was busy on the other side of the tent. After he made sure the guy was not paying attention to their conversation, he spoke barely above a whisper.

"I have this friend of mine who wants to be an outlaw, but I fear for his safety. It would be a good lesson if he could ride with you guys maybe for a small excursion of cattle rustling somewhere in New Mexico. That way he may truly understand what it's like to dodge the law."

Four Finger Jack stared at him and calmly asked, "Are you suggesting that we are cattle rustlers and should do something against the law to teach your friend the good and bad sides of riding the owl hoot trail? Are you pulling my donkey's tail? Why in the world should we risk ending in the calaboose for the sake of educating that saphead friend of yours?"

Hutchinson had expected that question. "Let's put it this way, the fellow is mighty rich, and I'm sure he would share some of his silver coins with you guys if he could ride your brand for a try. He is not the brightest candle and won't realize it is a set up excursion."

Now he'd gotten their full attention. Most people in this town forgot about their own safety when the call of silver tempted their grabby hearts. "Well, let's see, we could take him with us on a short raid for horses down at the border near Shakespeare, New Mexico. It is about time to earn a few dollars anyway. All right, box herder, when are we supposed to meet this tenderfoot friend of yours?"

"I will introduce him to you fellers in the evening. He will sit at his usual poker spot at the Bird Cage Theatre. I will also make sure that three of my ladies of the line welcome you in the proper way including some of the finest liquor in town."

Hours later Hutchinson walked over to Russian Bill's table and introduced the three saddle tramps to him. "Bill, these gentlemen are looking for a partner to accompany them for some business in Shakespeare, New Mexico. I want to be honest. It sounds like a mighty risky excursion but knowing your taste for dangerous adventures you might wanna talk with them." Hutchinson smiled at Russian Bill, but the smile did not reach his cold eyes. Russian Bill got up and followed the three men to a table in the corner not too far from the bar. Hutchinson watched the four men talking and held back the three girls until he saw the men shaking hands.

"Go, mosey on over to those gents over there and take a bottle of whiskey along. I want you to entertain them but don't get those scalawags drunk. They have to ride out of town tomorrow, and I don't want them to forget about their task."

The girls nodded. Of course, they knew that they would not succeed in seducing Russian Bill. It was an open secret that he had eyes for Mae Davenport only. The others of course would be easy prey.

William Tattenbaum had never tried to hide the fact that he admired the rebellious outlaws, but so far Curly Bill and his friends had never taken him seriously enough to let him join their gang. Here was his chance to become a real frontier longrider. He had often told Curly Bill that he wanted to be recognized and admired as a dangerous man. It was his dream to restore some of the respect and reputation he had had as an elite soldier of the Russian czar before he had to flee his home country.

After his conversation with the three outlaws, Russian Bill waited impatiently until Mae showed up for work and immediately told her that he was supposed to ride on an important mission to Shakespeare the following day.

Mae thought the story sounded somewhat fishy and unusual. Mae was less enthusiastic and didn't like at all that her lover was so thrilled about participating in a questionable mission far from Tombstone. She watched the three villains whom she had never seen before. There was something about them that gave her the chills. "Do you know these fellows?" she asked Russian Bill.

"Have never seen them," he answered with a shrug of his broad shoulders.

"So why did they approach you and not one of Clanton's boys. They know better about cattle or whatever they want you to herd with them."

"Most of the cowboys are not in town."

"I don't like any of this, Bill. Something doesn't sound right. Why don't you tell them to find someone else?" But he shook his head.

Every attempt to stop him from riding with the strangers failed. After spending a passionate night together in his quarters, both parted in the early dawn hours as the gray daylight slowly crawled over the Tombstone hills filled with silver.

"Please come back soon, my love," she whispered and held him tight. He kissed her gently and stroked her long hair as if to calm her.

"I promise to always return to you, Mae. Nobody can keep us apart, I swear."

Mae still felt his touch and lips on her skin when she arrived at the house which she shared with the other two girls. But apart from his sweet caress, she felt something else—fear.

An hour later the man who owned the most famous house of ill repute in town watched the four riders leave east bound. A satisfied, devilish grin showed on his face while he dropped the lace curtains back into place and turned away from the window of his front parlor.

CHAPTER 21

LOSING EVERYTHING

*M*ae was sad and restless that evening. Her performance on stage was well appreciated as usual, but she didn't entertain any men in the downstairs chamber. She couldn't pin it down, but something seemed suspicious about that sudden offer to her man to join those lowlifes. The gut feeling worried her throughout the whole night. She could always count on it. If only she knew what was wrong. Even after returning home, she paced back and forth in her room not finding any sleep.

"Bill is a grown-up man, Mae. He can take care of himself, believe me," Lizette said, wanting to calm her nervous friend.

"I know, Lizette, and I don't want to act like a mother hen, but something is off. I feel it in my heart. I am scared like never before in my life."

Mae tried to find a few hours of sleep but failed. The next day she was tired and worried. She went to the Bird Cage earlier than usual hoping that Bill might be back already. Instead, she ran into Curly Bill. He smiled at her and asked her right away why his friend had not appeared at the poker table.

"Did you wear out poor Bill so that he is too exhausted to show up for a round of poker? That would be the first time in months and speaks for your skills, if you know what I mean," he added with a boyish grin.

Mae was pale and shook her head. She didn't like Curly Bill and judged him as being a rather dangerous man. Since her arrival in Tombstone, she witnessed more than one hot-tempered discussion with the Earp brothers, who represented the law in Tombstone, and Curly Bill had never backed down. Mae wasn't sure if the guy feared anything, but one thing was certain, he did not respect the law dogs in this mining camp.

According to the employees at the Bird Cage, one was well advised not to get on his bad side, and Russian Bill agreed to that common opinion. "If someone tries to outsmart Curly Bill, he might as well deliver his measurements ahead to the undertaker before doing so," her lover had once whispered with a chuckle.

Despite fearing Curly Bill, Mae pulled herself together and told him about the weird incident of the mob of outlaws asking her lover out of the blue to join them. "It was not me keeping him away from the poker cards, Curly Bill. To be honest, I am sick with worry. He said he didn't know these villains but rode with them nevertheless. He said something about regaining the respect he once head in the old world. I cannot tell you what scares me, but I know that something is wrong about all this."

Curly Bill squinted his eyes and listened in silence. "All right, I admit I never took my Russian poker partner seriously as a *bandito*, but hey, I really like that dude. Who wouldn't? He is educated and good to talk to, not to forget the fun we have shuffling those cards together." Of course, he did not mention the fact that Russian Bill always carried enough money on him to provide not only himself but his friends a great time, too, at the Bird Cage Theatre.

"You are right, Mae. Something sounds wrong here, and I

don't like it either. I have a gut feeling what that so called mission might be, but nobody with brains worth two cents would take an unexperienced cattle rustler along."

"Oh my God, you think he rode with them to steal cattle?" Mae looked as if she were about to faint.

"Judging from the way you describe them, especially the fellow with a finger missing, my guessing is we are talking about Four Finger Jack and his brothers. Not a good gang to hang out with. I am not a saint myself, but these three are not very experienced in what they do and have the tendency to run into severe trouble."

"What can we do, Curly Bill? I fear for my man. I am not good when it comes to asking for help, but I am begging you to help your friend," Mae said with tears in her eyes.

Curly Bill studied her face for a moment. Then he sighed. "All right, all right, quit crying, woman. I will ride toward Shakespeare to find out what this was all about. Might take me two to three days though."

Mae was quite relieved. "I don't know how to thank you," she whispered. He shook his head.

"Listen, Mae, I don't do this very often, but Russian Bill is a man to ride the river with. I actually trust him, and believe me, that is not very often the case. As soon as I know more about his whereabouts, I will let you know. Besides, I do not accept it that some scamps are messing around in my territory."

She nodded and walked into the Bird Cage feeling somewhat relieved that Bill's friend would be looking for him.

The next three days passed, and Mae hadn't heard from Russian Bill neither from his friend or Four Finger Jack and his scalawags.

She was not her usual cheerful self and turned down most of the men who wanted to pay for her company. Hutchinson finally pulled her aside and made it clear that he wanted his guests to be entertained in the best possible way. "I am sorry, but I am just not feeling up to it," she replied when he stopped scolding her. But then the owner of the Bird Cage acted unexpectedly rude.

"Listen to me, you little dancing filly. You were hired to entertain the men in every way, whether you feel up to it or not. In case you're worried about your Russian lover, let me tell you, he probably forgot all about you already. I am sure he rode to the next boom town and is having fun in the arms of the next soiled dove," he added with a smirk.

Mae shook her head vehemently. "That's not true. He would never leave me behind like this."

Hutchinson laughed, but it was a mean sound. "Really, little dancing fawn? Is that so? Well, then let me tell you, I overheard him saying he was getting bored with you. Did you really think he was serious about you? Lord, look at you, girl. You sell your favors for silver. Now, show me one man who would have respectful thoughts about a woman with such easy morals." He shook his head, his arms crossed in front of his chest. He oozed off self-righteousness. "There wouldn't even be a single prospector in this town who would have serious intentions about spending the rest of his life with you. Russian Bill can have any woman in this house or at Devil's Addiction on Sixth Street. And believe me, he's laid numerous of those painted cats already," Hutchinson added with cruel laughter.

His words hurt as if he had slapped her in the face. *Is this true? Does this dirty bastard know something I don't?* Doubts flared up like a burning flame. After all, Hutchinson had known her beloved Bill much longer than she had.

Mae turned and walked through the front door. She was furious and heartbroken. *What if he is right?* It was possible, wasn't it?

Now that she had thought about it, Bill had not dropped the idea of riding with that gang, although she had been sick with worry. Maybe he really didn't care for her. *What in the world did you expect,* she scolded herself. *I should have known better. I should have listened to Peter's warning. I should have stayed with the carnival.*

Blinded by tears, she took a few steps on the boardwalk and bumped right into Curly Bill's chest.

"Whoa, hold your horses, little dancing queen, where are you going?"

"Curly Bill! Oh, my goodness, am I relieved to see you."

He laughed. "Dang! It must be over a decade since I've heard a beautiful woman say that."

But then his face changed immediately, and he looked rather serious. He took her arm and pulled her to the other side of the road so the guests who were drinking and talking in front of the Theatre's entrance couldn't overhear their conversation. Some of the men stared at the two of them, but everyone pretended not to pay much attention. No one in town dared to interfere in Curly Bill's business.

CHAPTER 22

THE CRUEL TRUTH

"What happened? What's wrong? Where is my man?" Mae could barely hold back her fear. She knew something was wrong and saw it in Curly Bill's eyes.

The feared gunslinger did not lower his gaze but looked into her eyes, then he cleared his throat. Curly Bill Brocius hesitated, looking to find the right words, and for the first time in many years, he tried to avoid sounding heartless.

"The cowboys Russian Bill rode with were foolish enough to steal some horses from a cattle baron who has quite a few ranch hands. They immediately set up a posse. Four Finger Jack shot one of them, and the posse followed them all the way back to the border of the Arizona territory. They caught Pete, Jeff, and Russian Bill. Four Finger Jack escaped. The bloody jerk left his men and even his brother behind to save his own neck from the hangman."

Mae covered her face with her hands. "So, he's in prison now? Oh goodness, what a mess. When is the trial?"

Brocius shook his head. "Unfortunately, the ranch hand that

got shot was the rancher's son. They gathered a mob, whipped them into a fury, and...."

Mae stared at him not wanting to hear the rest. "What are you trying to say?" she whispered.

"Sweet Jesus, how do I tell this?" Curly Bill whispered, raking his hands through his black hair in despair. He wasn't good at tiptoeing around people's feelings, so he tried to get over with it as fast as possible.

"Believe me, Mae, I tried my best, but there was no stopping them. It was a hell of a nasty crowd. There was even a law dog among the posse, but the cattle rancher threatened him with a shotgun. Looks like he has a lot to say in that area. By God, I swear they would have put the sheriff six feet under if he had tried to protect them prisoners. It would have been suicide to step in between the mob and the captured cattle thieves. You should have heard Pete. He was cursing Hutchinson like crazy," Curly Bill added as if he were trying to win time to spill the devastating news.

"Curly Bill, where is my man?" Mae asked through the tears streaming down her cheeks.

"I am sorry, my dear, but I have to tell you that he's dead. They hung him along with the other two fellows. I wished I could have helped him, but it would have been straight suicide, and nobody would have ever changed the mob's opinion about him or the others. The man didn't have the slightest chance. But at least he did not suffer. The rope snapped his neck like a dead branch off a tree when he fell. Bill was dead immediately."

Mae stared at him. She tried to grasp the words but couldn't accept their meaning. She was sure William Tattenbaum—known to all of them as Russian Bill—would ride around the corner onto Allen Street at any moment.

She thought this must be some sort of bad joke. As she glared at Curly Bill Brocius, finally the words pierced her consciousness like painful daggers. "What are you saying? He cannot be dead. That is not possible. He was here with me only three days ago, and there was no talk about cattle rustling when he decided to ride with those villains." She was heartbroken and stared at the outlaw who gazed down to his boots. "He cannot be hung. Why would anybody hang my man? He has not harmed anybody." She started to shiver and sobbed as tears streamed freely now.

He was gone. The man she loved deeply and had wanted to spend the rest of her life with would never return into her loving arms. But then, through the worst pain she ever experienced in her born days, something Curly Bill had mentioned tugged at her consciousness.

"What did you mean when you said Pete cursed Hutchinson? Why? What has that pimp got to do with all of this?"

The famous gunman looked toward the notorious theatre, his face changing into a dangerously controlled mask, his eyes glittering with hatred.

"He apparently had set Four Finger Jack and his saddle tramps up to lure Russian Bill out of town for a few days."

"What? Why in the world would he do that? He earns a lot of money from Bill who pays him at least twenty silver dollars every night for that one booth next to the stage." She stared at the outlaw, not understanding at all what he was trying to tell her.

"You don't get it, do you? That rat loses much more money if his poker-playing client seduces one of his painted ladies to fly into the marriage nest and to give up performing her trade in that hell hole over there. That would be a true loss for him. You're one of the best ponies in the stable since you stayed back when your circus friends left. Just recall the unbelievable amount your lover Bill paid for one night with you."

Mae blushed. "He told you?" She was deeply embarrassed. The gunslinger simply nodded.

"There is no reason to be ashamed. Bill was a gentleman of the first water. To find true love is priceless, my dancing fawn."

The devastated calico queen stared into Curly Bill's face and finally understood what he indicated. Her lips trembled, and her eyes grew huge with disbelief.

"It was because of me, wasn't it? Hutchinson pulled that nasty trick because of me. My love for Bill has literally killed him. Is that what you're trying to tell me?"

Her pitch had risen, and she became frenzied. It was known in town that hysterical women were something Curly Bill couldn't stand at all, but this time he didn't walk away. Instead, he embraced her as a caring friend, and at that moment it looked as if he understood how close his poker chap Bill and the dancing carnival girl Mae Davenport had really been.

"Yes, you truly loved him, didn't you? At first, I thought you were after his money or the good looks that spark had, but there was more to it, wasn't it? Dang, I even envy that fool for having found the precious gift of true love," he whispered while he held the sobbing woman close to his broad chest.

"Of course, you should never let anybody know that. After all, I am Curly Bill Brocius, one of the leaders of the cowboy gang in Cochise County. Folks should continue fearing my name. Don't tell anybody that I was jealous of this feller's luck with the dancing fawn."

She scoffed and rubbed her sleeve over her wet cheeks. "Thank you for riding out there. Looks like you have been a true friend to my beloved Bill."

"Mae, I need to tell you something else." She slowly turned her gaze upward, her expression a mask of pure pain.

"When Russian Bill spotted me in the crowd, he begged me to come closer, and I did. He told me to let you know that he'll come back to you."

She shook her head. "He's dead for God's sake! Why would

he say such a thing with a rope around his neck? What kind of cruel gimmick is that?"

"I don't know, Mae. I really don't know." He tried to calm her, and guilt was written all over his face for not having been able to save his friend's life. How ironic it was that Russian Bill had died a real outlaw's death although everybody had just made fun of him as a wannabe villain.

Suddenly she jerked away from him and walked briskly across the street toward the theatre's entrance. He was surprised by her unexpected move and stood across the Bird Cage, a confused expression clouding his tough features.

CHAPTER 23

THE CURSE

*S*tanding in the doorway of the town's most famous honky-tonk, Mae screamed Hutchinson's name over and over as if she had lost her mind.

Curly Bill wondered what she was up to and took a step across the street to follow her, when his hand touched his belt and he realized that his big knife was gone from the scabbard.

"Dang! The crazy woman must have snatched my Bowie." He crossed the street as fast as he could but had to jump back, startled by the noises of a stagecoach that rolled by, moving quickly. When the path to the premises across the street cleared, he ran over, afraid she would try to hurt the despicable villain with his knife. Not that Curly Bill cared much for Hutchinson, but after all, it was his blade she was planning to use. He'd had enough trouble lately with those Earp brothers and their self-proclaimed tin star justice and didn't need more of it.

"You took everything away from me, Hutchinson! Where are you, you greedy bastard! He was a good friend to you, paid you a fortune, and you? This is how you thank your pal and best-paying regular guest? It was you who set up Russian Bill with a bunch of scalawags to lure my man into a deadly trap!" Mae was madder than a hornet, and when she spotted Hutchinson in the crowd, she shook her left fist at him. Conversations had died down around them, and even the piano music stopped playing after the player realized that all the attention had turned toward the long bar for some reason. A hush went through the guests when they heard the accusations yelled into the face of the box herder. "What is she talking about?" one of the barkeepers whispered from behind the bar's counter.

The owner of the establishment looked around nervously, his rat-like eyes darting from one corner to the other, but his guests had encircled him making an escape impossible. It seemed that everybody inside the theatre waited for his explanation to set the record straight.

For the first time since he was the owner of this place, Hutchinson's face showed fear. This whole intrigue had gotten out of hand. Of course, he had never wanted his best-paying guest to get lynched by a mob. After all, it was known that the love-crazy fool had paid Hutchinson a fortune for his poker table every single night.

And now his own dirty games backfired and left him with a hysterical prostitute screaming at him. The crowd gasped when Mae started to raise a big Bowie knife in her right hand, the blade reflecting some of the light of the chandeliers in the room.

To Hutchinson's surprise, nobody laid hands on the woman who had obviously gone crazy. Although the crowd appreciated the entertainment provided in the Bird Cage Theatre every day and night, the owner was known for his greediness, and the guests were quite fond of Mae as well as Russian Bill. Everybody stood still as if hypnotized and wanted to hear the woman out. Even his employees stood behind the bar, their arms crossed over the chest and obviously wondered if Mae was speaking the truth.

Hutchinson knew that if the reality of his dirty dealings to harm that gambler's liaison with one of his girls became known among his guests and in town, he would surely lose a lot of money. The situation was dangerous for his reputation and business. Some of Russian Bill's friends might even try to take revenge for the gambler's death.

The pimp tried to calm the furious woman, raising his hands in self-defense. "Mae, believe me, I have nothing to do with all of this. I don't even know what you are talking about."

"You're a bloody liar. You're nothing but a varmint who abuses women," she screamed at the top of her lungs. "There was a witness, right there when they hung my Bill. You are responsible for the death of Russian Bill, your partners in crime admitted it when they had a noose around their necks. I curse you, Hutchinson! I lost everything and may be going to hell, but I will take you with me even if it is the last thing I do. You shall be damned to stay in this god-forsaken brothel of yours for eternity. You shall never be free, you hear me? Never! May the devil keep you prisoner in this cursed building of yours and at no time let your soul find peace."

Mae raised the big knife high above her head, the lights flashing off its sharp blade. Clutching Hutchinson's collar with a final scream that had the onlookers' hairs standing up, she brought down the Bowie knife with one fast slash. Curly Bill tried to stop her, yelling, "Mae, don't," but he didn't reach the rage-blinded woman in time to succeed.

The sickening sound of metal ripping through fabric and flesh seemed unusually loud. The nearby men stood in disbelief, paralyzed for a few seconds. All they saw was Hutchinson and Mae going down, the corpulent man lying on the ground and tiny Mae beneath his bloated body.

After a few seconds, the crowd reacted and pushed the overweight man off of the slender dancer's body. Everybody expected him to be seriously wounded, but then the shocked people saw that Mae lay on the hardwood floor with the knife stuck in her abdomen, her right hand still holding its wooden grip. "Did she fall into the blade?" a man whispered.

"Stupid fool," Curly Bill yelled. "She killed herself. Lord, have mercy on her soul."

A dark stain started to spread on Mae's lovely dress, and she blinked her tears away. She heard Lizette screaming from somewhere behind the row of men staring down at her. The iron-like smell of fresh blood battled against the cigar smoke of the onlookers standing next to the dying woman. Mae raised a bloody hand and touched Hutchinson's face almost tenderly. Her soft whisper was only meant to be heard by him and Curly Bill, who had knelt down beside her.

"I condemn you, William Hutchinson. May your greed hold you prisoner in this theatre of yours forever." She smeared her blood onto the man's face. He frantically scrambled back, his face a mask of pure horror. A shocked hush fell over the crowd. Some crossed themselves.

The man was cursed by a woman who had committed the deadly sin of suicide, not willing to live without the love of her life. Her breathing came shallow now, and the stain of blood grew like a blossom of death. Mae's eyes locked with those of Curly Bill who didn't dare to touch his own knife.

"He will come back, right? He promised, you said," she whispered.

The gunfighter kneeled next to her and slowly nodded his head. He looked serious, and it was easy to see that his heart was filled with sorrow for the dying beauty. "You loved each other deeply. You will find each other again, little dancing fawn," he whispered.

She managed a small, shy smile. Then her eyes went blank, staring at the ceiling, no longer seeing the countless bullet holes which had worried her during her first performance at the famous Bird Cage Theatre a lifetime ago. Mae's pretty head rolled gently to the side. The hardwood floor soaked up her blood, leaving a dark stain in the wood.

Mae Davenport would never dance at the Bird Cage again. She had left the theatre for good, but her curse would remain right there within the famous walls.

CHAPTER 24

THE SHADOWS OF YESTERYEAR

*C*heryl opened her eyes and realized that she sat in the rocking chair on the front porch of her temporary home in Tombstone. She couldn't remember having fallen asleep or how long she had been out. It was dark, and she felt cold.

She still wore the green dress Dorothea had given to her and felt depressed. A pang of great loss had her on the edge of crying. Cheryl rose and walked into the house. This time she remembered every detail of her dream, and a sadness like she had never known almost choked her. She sobbed as she undressed and crawled under the covers, feeling cold despite the cozy quilt she covered herself with.

When Cheryl arrived at work the following day, Dorothea was shocked at how pale and tired Cheryl looked. Dark circles showed under her eyes, which were bloodshot as if she had cried for hours.

"Girl, what's the matter with you? Did yesterday's events scare the wits out of you? You look as if you've seen a ghost or something."

The younger woman shrugged her shoulders. "Well, I guess

that's exactly what happened. I saw Russian Bill, or more accurately, he paid me a visit. He's the one whose voice and cherry cigar smoke follows me all around town. Frankly, I'm quite sure I'm losing my mind."

Dorothea poured her friend a fresh cup of coffee. It was a weekday, and the museum hadn't been busy the past few days.

"What exactly has happened, and what do you mean by you saw Russian Bill?"

Cheryl sat down, stifled a yawn, and told Dorothea everything, including her dream about Mae's tragic death. When she finished, her heart was pounding so hard in her chest that she was pretty sure her motherly friend could hear it.

The older lady remained silent for a moment, and by the shaking of her head Cheryl guessed that Dorothea was surprised at how fast events had developed since their evening together. The story of Mae Davenport committing suicide before the front bar of the Bird Cage was extremely unnerving.

Dorothea knew that certain men had been killed over a deck of cards or during a heated argument among the miners and buckaroos in that building. She had told Cheryl all about it during one of their lunch breaks. Therefore, it was not astonishing that people thought that the building was haunted.

But this death had a different outcome with Mister Hutchinson being damned. "I wonder if Mae's curse is still active," Dorothea mumbled. "If so, it might be the reason why Hutchinson's restless soul still tries to call women back to work as ladies of the night."

"Is it possible that the theatre continues to exist as a notorious gambling place and brothel despite being turned into a museum decades ago?" Cheryl asked her friend. The thought seemed outrageous.

"Whatever happened there, one thing is sure— the events of the past few weeks have had an impact on you, and I am starting to worry for your safety, Cheryl." Dorothea's face showed her concern. "This is going way beyond anything my husband or I have experienced in Tombstone so far. I want to be honest, girl. I don't like what's happening here." Cheryl didn't feel good about it either. Everything she experienced in this town stood against common sense.

That evening back in her guest house, the California student ate a sandwich, although she didn't feel hungry at all. She couldn't say what was wrong with her, but since that terrible dream the night before, she felt an extreme sensation of loss and a longing for the man whose shadowy figure she had seen standing on her porch.

Cheryl didn't question what was happening in this weird little Western town any longer. Deep inside of her subconsciousness she knew that she belonged here and that her life in California would never be the same if she returned there.

She showered, dressed in her favorite sweatshirt, and curled up on the couch. She tried to distract herself and zapped through all of the TV channels, but her thoughts returned to the unhappy ending of the frontier love story. Frustrated, she turned the set off.

All of the movies and shows seemed too loud, too annoying, so she lit the petroleum lamp and turned off the lights in the kitchen and living room.

Now, that's better. She picked up the second book that she bought a few days ago. But nothing occupied her concentration long enough to stop her thoughts from traveling back to the masculine figure and handsome face of Russian Bill's spirit, and she caught herself trying to recall the sound of his voice whispering to her.

Oh my God, I wonder what making love to him would be like. I don't believe in ghosts, and here I go fantasizing about the spirit of an 1880s gambler. Oh girl, how ridiculous is that.

"Mae, why do you doubt what you see with your own eyes? Why don't you accept what you hear with your own ears?"

Where in the world did that voice come from right here in the house?

"Darling, do you really think that walls could be a boundary for me when I can easily pass the distance of a hundred and thirty-six years?"

Cheryl closed her eyes for an instant. "Bill, is that you?" she asked with a timid voice.

The answer came immediately as a cool breeze gently touched her right cheek. It felt like the caress of a feather. Soon she saw his shadow sitting next to her. She wanted to reach out with her hand, but he motioned her to stop.

"Mae, I am in the dark world of the shadows. You are here in the future Tombstone with your flesh and blood—so warm, so alive. We cannot be together until you cross from your world to the other side."

"What do you mean? Explain it to me, please." But he was vanishing like the fog on a cold fall day. She tried to hold him back and sobbed, "Please, Bill! Come back. Explain it to me."

But he was gone, and Cheryl was left behind, lonely and confused in the small house that had belonged to Crazy Anne during a period of time Cheryl didn't understand much about.

The next few days passed without anything unusual happening, and she was caught in the familiar routine of museum work and meeting people in Tombstone.

By now Cheryl was considered a member of the local population, although everybody knew she planned to return to California in late October.

Cheryl looked at Tombstone very differently now compared to the first few days of her stay. Okay, she admitted that there were some real weirdos living in town, and it seemed like some folks were stuck in their life of reenactment. Countless people in this Western settlement appeared to have given up their true identity, and some actually seemed as if they had never had an identity of their own to start with. Cheryl was also aware of the many alcoholics and crystal meth addicts and felt sorry for them.

Without realizing it, an acceptance for the dark side of Tombstone had found its place in Cheryl's heart.

CHAPTER 25

THE OLD MORGUE

On her day off she strolled up and down Allen Street but tried her best to avoid the eerie historical brothel. Why, she didn't know for sure, but it had to do with the growling voice that had called her back to work the other day and which still made her shiver with fear when she thought of it.

Cheryl passed a shop next to the creepy building which she had never noticed before. As she walked by the entrance door, someone called her name.

"Cheryl, would you wait a second?"

She stopped in her tracks, surprised that the lady walking toward her from the back of the store knew her name. But then this was Tombstone, a small-town community, so she shouldn't really be surprised about it.

"Hi there, sorry to holler at you like that. I'm Nora." The lady with the dark, gray-streaked hair shook her hand.

"Cheryl. Pleasure to meet you. What can I do for you?"

"Would you join me in the store for a minute? I'll explain it to you," Nora said pointing inside.

She followed the storekeeper but felt a little uncomfortable.

When they reached a small lounge area in the back of the shop, the lady offered her a cup of coffee.

The store displayed refreshments and souvenirs in the front part of the building, but the back area was filled with sage, pendulums, tarot cards, and a tee-shirt rack.

What a weird mixture, Cheryl thought. She saw a door going off to the left and wondered what was behind it. *Most likely a staff toilet,* she mused.

"Wrong. It's the entrance to the part of the structure known as the old morgue," Nora said as she handed Cheryl a Styrofoam cup of steaming coffee. "Help yourself with sugar and creamer if you need any."

Cheryl stared at the woman. How in the world did Nora know that she thought it was the toilet? Nora pointed to the door.

"Most people come here to do paranormal investigations. A lot of them wonder about this door when they come here. The reason why the tourists book the tours through the old morgue is the fact that the place is pretty active even during the daytime. The shop is only a side business."

Oh, crap, Cheryl thought. That was all she needed right now. *Here you go, a shopping trip to the haunted morgue.* But she didn't want to be rude. So, she sipped her coffee and waited for Nora's explanation as to why she had called her into the place.

"As I said, in the old days, this was a full-time morgue. Enough killings happened daily in Tombstone, and that kept the undertakers real busy," Nora explained.

"They had at least two or three full-time morticians working here. Imagine, busy San Francisco at that time had only one undertaker. There was another structure between the Bird Cage and us, but that's long gone. Our building is a paranormal hot spot so to speak, so we offer ghost tours daily."

The owner of the place saw Cheryl's face full of doubts and

pointed to the back of the shop. "Come with me, and you'll understand." She put down her own coffee cup and walked toward the cream-colored, wooden door. It opened to a small, rustic bar area and a bigger room which looked like a compact indoor theatre.

Cheryl walked along the hardwood floor that creaked under her shoes and studied the pictures on the walls. She saw a big red curtain that was used to block out the daylight. The atmosphere was chilly, and the student felt as if she were being watched. But that was, of course, nonsense, she told herself. Nora looked at her.

"Last night we did a late-night session, and during that paranormal investigation your name was mentioned by a spirit called Crazy Anne. She used to be one of the Bird Cage girls, but from the look on your face, I assume you already know very well who Crazy Anne is, don't you?"

Cheryl swallowed but could not speak. Instead, she nodded.

"Take a seat, please," Nora said and motioned to the simple chairs around a big, round table.

Since Cheryl was off from work with no appointments to rush to, she sat down. The room was gloomy. *Bright daylight most likely would not be appropriate in an old morgue,* Cheryl assumed. Nora regarded her with her almond-shaped gray eyes, and her face showed a serious expression.

"I reckon you don't know much about paranormal activities, right?"

"Jesus, I don't even know if I should believe the things I see with my own eyes lately, to be frank," Cheryl exclaimed. She let her hands fall back into her lap in a helpless gesture.

"I see. Well, let me explain," the friendly lady said. "Most people think in the past, present, or future contexts, which is generally correct. But what they don't know is that past and present are in existence on a parallel level."

"How is that possible?" Cheryl asked.

Nora placed two strips of photo negatives on the table.

"We think way too one-dimensionally. But the world and life are multidimensional, in the sense that the past doesn't necessarily have to end because the present has started. As a matter of fact, the past still exists. At least, for the spirits it does. They contact us here in the present day, but many of them actually still live in their old times and in their old lives. Some of them don't know or don't accept that their living days are over."

"That's crazy. Simply not possible."

Cheryl felt as if Nora was pulling her leg, yet she knew that the woman was describing an astonishing event that she had been witnessing herself lately.

As the shop owner continued, she had Cheryl's full attention. "There are places in this world that are hot spots for paranormal activity. We call them 'Crossovers' or 'Gateways.' It could be a battlefield, an area where a disaster had occurred, or a building, for instance. People often think that the cemeteries are the most haunted places. But they're actually not.

"Instead, it's the places where people have lived or died to which their restless souls may return. See these two negatives?" She pointed to the strips on the table. "A paranormal gateway is similar to the two negatives. When I put one on top of the other, both pictures shine through, not completely and not clearly, but visible to both sides."

Cheryl nodded. Nora's explanation made some sort of sense, yet it was still against the science Cheryl had grown up with.

Nora pointed at the two stripes of negatives. "This is what happens at such hot spots, and it's exactly what's going on at the Bird Cage Theatre, as well as here at the morgue. It's as if the mirror of the present time becomes a transparent veil which gives us a small glimpse into the past, and a few gifted people can actually not only look through that veil but also communicate with the other side. But a gateway is a crossover that works both ways to a certain extent. That is the reason why some among us are able to see or hear the ones on the other side. Crazy Anne told me last night that Russian Bill calls you because you may be Cheryl in this modern time, but your body seems to hold the soul of the woman formerly known as Mae Davenport."

Cheryl shook her head. Her common sense blocked her from believing the obvious. "You know what I think? I believe everybody in this town has gone wacko believing all this crazy stuff."

Cheryl was about to rush out of the room when the weird lady called her back. Her voice was calm and barely above a whisper.

"He wanted so much to stay and to feel your touch last night but couldn't. He is still caught on the other side of the mirror, and only a living person can cross to the side of the past for good. Russian Bill is a prisoner in the world of shadows. But he said he felt your hand reaching out to him yesterday."

"How do you know about last night?" Cheryl whispered. *This isn't possible, or is it?*

The storekeeper ignored her question and said, "I hope you understand what that means. There's no way Russian Bill can be with you as long as you are alive. But I have no doubt that you are indeed the re-incarnated Mae Davenport."

Cheryl stared at the woman who slowly got up and walked back to the door to the main store. She followed her, cup in her hand but long forgotten. The younger visitor was confused but thanked Nora and promised to come back for one of the evening tours soon.

Cheryl walked to her accommodation and didn't pay attention to any of the people walking or driving by. Nora's words suddenly hit home. "He can never be with you as long as you are alive. Only the living can cross to the other side for good."

Cheryl felt as if she had lost her lover a second time and couldn't do anything to fix it. Why do I miss him with such a yearning and a physical hunger unlike anything I have ever experienced before? What did it feel like for Mae when they made love? How would it be for me to sleep with him?

If only he were alive. Could she come to terms with the thought that she might be the reborn Mae Davenport or that a former lover had returned as a ghost to bring her back home? *Am I losing my mind here in this god-forsaken, dusty town?*

Without thinking twice, Cheryl decided to return to the shop called Paranormal Sisters for an evening appointment of ghost hunting at the old morgue. She grabbed her phone to call the number on the card Nora had given her as she had to find more answers.

The friendly lady signed her up for the late-hour group after 10:00 p.m. and said how thrilled she was that Cheryl would be joining them.

CHAPTER 26

PARANORMAL INVESTIGATION

*W*alking back to the old morgue, she knew that she had to get up early for work the following day but didn't mind. At 9:30 p.m., she stepped through the door and smelled a bad sulfur odor like rotten eggs. That disgusting smell hadn't been there in the afternoon, and Cheryl wrinkled her nose in dismay. Nora noticed it right away.

"You smell it too, don't you?"

"Yeah, what in the world is it?"

Nora looked toward the other room. "Some spirits are pretty evil. They carry a stench like that. The morgue seems to be outstandingly active tonight. The eight o'clock tour was so full of activity that one lady had a panic attack and left, literally running out of here. Guess she's over at Doc Holliday's bar now trying to recover from her shock. This stuff can freak some people out."

They both laughed, but Cheryl felt quite insecure. About ten minutes later, another four tourists walked into the place. They all had booked the same tour and were pretty excited, chatting nervously. When the group was complete, Nora locked the front door and turned on an emergency light. All other lights had to be switched off. Their host welcomed the group and led them into the adjoining room.

Nora explained the history of the morgue and how rowdy the past had been during the silver boom years. "In Tombstone's heydays we had two to three full-time morticians working here. San Francisco, which was considerably huge by that time, didn't have half the numbers of undertakers. As a matter of fact, Tombstone had two morgues."

Nora showed them a small room in the back. "This is where the dead bodies were drained of blood and embalmed. See the opening in the roof which looks like a chimney?" Everybody nodded. "That opening was a lifesaver. The embalming fluid contained arsenic, and we all know how deadly it can be to handle that toxic chemical. Those days they were not aware of it, at least not to the same degree as they do today."

The group walked into the small area with the crude bar and a big antic mirror behind it. Next to the bar was an old piece of furniture which looked like a foldable table. Nora pointed to it. "This, ladies and gentlemen, is one of the original mortician tables used in the old days. When we took over this place, we found a lot of items. The wooden box underneath this foldable table contains numerous bottles with the original embalming liquid. We found it in the basement."

Everybody stared at the old wooden box filled with square bottles. Nora pulled out one of them and pointed to the amber-colored liquid.

"We were pretty lucky to have found a lot of the original equipment still stored in this building."

At the end of the informational tour, Nora led the group into the main room across the small rustically built bar and asked everyone to sit down around the big table. "In the old days someone died in this town every day. Now remember, most of the folks here were fortune hunters and miners. Some of the dead bodies found were unknown, and the undertakers would showcase the body over there in the big window placed in a special coffin with a glass lid for at least three days."

A young guy wearing sneakers, shorts, and a baseball cap raised his hand. Nora motioned him to speak. "Now, why in the world would they display the body in the window?" the youngster wanted to know.

"Good question. If the deceased were unknown, the undertakers had nobody who would pay for the funeral or the coffin and embalming. Therefore, they tried to find people who knew the person by showing him or her to the public hoping that someone would volunteer to pay for their services."

Cheryl felt a chill when she pictured an unknown body in a casket being exposed to everybody walking up and down the boardwalk. The one thing it always came down to was that quite often in life money was more important than human dignity. That hadn't changed at all.

Nora walked from chair to chair and handed out different electronic devices. "These items will let us know if there is a sudden change of temperature or some sort of magnetic energy or unusual electrical static. You have probably seen them in some of the TV shows about the paranormal. I also have a voice recorder hooked up to my computer and speakers to increase the sound of whispers we might hear. Sometimes the radio station in Sierra Vista interferes a bit because these devices are super sensitive to any energy swing, so if you hear a lively rock song, then it is not a message from the 1880s."

Everybody laughed nervously while Nora placed one flashlight on the table and one on the mortician's furniture, which stood a few feet away from the seated visitors. She switched them on, and the way they were placed, nobody was able to touch them from where everybody sat. The host of the tour started her laptop and logged in on her voice recorder program.

The laptop screen cast a ghostly light on Nora's face as she spoke into the silent room.

"Hello, ladies and gentlemen of the building. We want to greet you as respectful visitors. We hope that you wish to communicate with us today."

Cheryl had her doubts that this exercise would work the way it was expected. She was still extremely skeptical about the whole topic of ghost hunting. But then she recalled the weird evening when she and Dorothea had tried to contact Crazy Anne's spirit who had actually spoken to them. At least she believed that it was Crazy Anne.

As Cheryl's thoughts wandered, the flashlight on the table started flickering, and the light died. *The battery is probably done for the day.*

They could see the mortician's table through the connecting doorway into the adjoining room. A nervous hush went through the group when they witnessed how the second flashlight slowly rolled back and forth over the surface of the table. The light started to flicker as well and died.

An excited murmur rose among the group. Nora kept calling those spirits whom she identified as regular ghosts of the morgue. A crackling sound came from the laptop speakers. At first Cheryl thought it must be static distortion of some kind, but then single words spoken by different voices could be heard. Suddenly Cheryl recognized the voice of an angry man. It sounded like the growl of a dangerous animal, and she knew she had heard it before. Goosebumps covered her arms, and her heart pounded so hard she was sure the others must hear it.

Over and over again she heard him say the words, "She cursed me."

Nora asked the voice. "Who cursed you?"

"It was her. Mae."

Cheryl whispered into Nora's ear, "Is this Hutchinson?" but the older woman shrugged her shoulders. There were giggles of a woman, the rowdy laughter of another male voice, and then the one voice Cheryl would have recognized anywhere. *It must be him, Russian Bill,* she thought.

"Mae, come back to me."

She swallowed hard. Do the others hear that, too, or is the voice in my head?

Russian Bill. He called her, and immediately she felt her cheeks blush, and her heart skipped a beat or two.

Nora watched her closely, her face looked rather worried.

The other tourists in the group started to ask questions, but except for single words of which some of them were barely understandable, no further answers came. After around thirty minutes, Nora called the session off. She turned on the lights and guided everybody back to the main exit. The others gave Nora a tip and then left through the front store, chatting excitedly. They obviously experienced what they had expected for their money. For them it was a kind of game, a touristy thing to do.

Nora motioned Cheryl to stay back while she said goodbye to the other guests and thanked them for participating. "If you liked the Paranormal Sisters' tour, leave a nice review on Facebook or even better on TripAdvisor. It sure helps our business," she added.

Nora turned around and lit some sage she took from a metal bowl standing behind the counter. The white smoke which rose from the bundle spread a pleasant smell in the shop. To her surprise ,Nora fanned the smoke all over Cheryl and mumbled what sounded like some sort of prayer, which Cheryl didn't understand.

When Nora saw Cheryl's confused expression, she put the rest of the gleaming sage back into the metal bowl. "Sage helps for spiritual cleansing. It is important to use it after communicating with the spirits."

"But why didn't you light up sage for the others? Why only for me?" Cheryl asked.

"Simply because you were the target of the spirits who we heard today. By the way, I believe that the angry sounding one was indeed Hutchinson, but there was another spirit standing behind you, a handsomely shaped figure, as far as I could tell from his shadow. I smelled cherry cigars on him. He was the reason Hutchinson could not attack you any further. You recognized your protector's voice, didn't you?"

Cheryl looked away, sadness written all over her pretty features. "Yes," she whispered. "I think it was Russian Bill."

"I thought as much," Nora said. She turned around and turned off the lights in the glass cases. "Well, time to close this place up and go home. In case you have any questions or want to come back again for a chat, with me or maybe with *them*, you know where to find us all."

Cheryl thanked Nora and slowly walked out of the building. As she glanced to the right, the Bird Cage Theatre hovered at the end of Allen Street like a dark spider waiting for a victim in its web.

She was bewildered. On the one hand, the place pulled her toward its entrance, and she sensed the once so happy days of the past inside. On the other, the building scared her since she faced those strange visions she could not control, especially since she knew that Mae died by her own hand during the tragic events that took place in 1882.

Cheryl turned around, watched Nora lock the door, and

waved goodnight. She strolled slowly along the deserted street toward her Victorian home.

Without being aware of it, Cheryl waited until she smelled the tobacco flavor she had gotten so used to during the past weeks. She was not at all worried when she saw a second shadow trailing her on Allen Street on her way to the little Victorian house. She knew it was Russian Bill's spirit, and his presence warmed her as she walked in the chilly air through the darkness of the Tombstone night.

When Cheryl arrived home, she looked over to the shadow and whispered, "I know you are not able to touch me, and sadly I can't feel you either. But maybe you can find a way to be with me in my sleep. Wouldn't that be possible in my dreams? They say that the spirits of lost loved ones can visit us while we sleep. Could you?"

He looked back at her, his face still blurry like a wavering picture, but she saw his smile. "My beloved Mae, I will try. Some days we can pass into today's world and be with those who we love. Some days we cannot. It is not true that spirits cannot touch the ones alive. As a matter of fact, evil spirits can even harm those who they attack. But in my case, I have to wait until you understand and accept that your body holds Mae's soul. As long as your heart is full of doubts you are unreachable for me. Being with you is only possible if you open your heart for me."

Cheryl nodded, but her heart felt heavy. She looked at him, but the shadow was vanishing, blown away by the cold breeze that came from the mountain's side.

She walked into the house and showered. The day at the morgue had exhausted her, and she went to bed without eating. Her sleep was rather a tossing-and-turning matter, and again and again she heard Hutchinson's angry voice blaming her for cursing him.

Despite being tired to the bone, she woke a couple of times

covered in her own cold sweat. Finally, long after 3:00 a.m., she fell into a deep slumber. And then Russian Bill found his way to enter her dreams and to make her feel his warm embrace and caresses through the barrier of time like it used to be in the old days.

CHAPTER 27

WORRIED FRIENDS

*N*ora returned to the old morgue the next morning and called Dorothea right away. She told her about the events of the paranormal session the previous night. "Dorothea, listen, you and I both know that this town is haunted, and for some reason your trainee girl triggers off events like crazy. I have never seen the place so active before. You should have heard Hutchinson's voice. It came through the speakers loud and clear."

"What are you getting at, Nora?" Dorothea asked. There was an instance of silence on the other side. When Nora spoke again, her voice was barely above a whisper.

"I believe that Cheryl is in grave danger. I think she should leave town, the faster the better. It is not Russian Bill I am concerned about, but Hutchinson worries me, and I am scared that another young woman might disappear."

Dorothea gasped. "Are you referring to Lisa? The police gave up on the search claiming that she most likely ran off with some other guy. To be honest I highly doubt that theory."

"So do I," Nora said. "I cannot tell you what it is, but I sense something evil growing inside the Bird Cage Theatre. The vibrations I get from that building are far from the normal paranormal activity. Something is brewing in there, and I am afraid that Cheryl is the key to it."

Dorothea looked very worried. "Nora, do you believe that our Cheryl is the re-incarnated Mae Davenport?"

"I have no doubt at all," Nora answered without hesitation.

"Let's meet for coffee in a few minutes. I will ask Bert to open the museum this morning. There is something I need to tell you but not over the phone."

"All right, come on over. Coffee will be ready in a few minutes."

Dorothea quickly explained to Bert that she needed to see Nora, and he agreed to take over the early morning shift at the Courthouse Museum. Just like Dorothea he was concerned about all the weird things that had happened during the last few days. Bert knew that certain things in Tombstone were not easily explained, but this was far beyond what he and his wife had experienced since moving into this town.

Less than twenty minutes later Dorothea walked into the Paranormal Sisters shop. Nora opened her business later than the stores and therefore locked the door again after Dorothea had arrived.

"Coffee with creamer, right?"

Dorothea nodded. "Yes, please." She took the Styrofoam cup and cradled it with both hands to warm her cold fingers.

Nora was not the kind of person who beat around the bush. "Okay, what's the matter?"

Dorothea took a sip of the hot beverage. "That warms my insides. Still cannot help the chill though," she added and looked cautiously at the door to the adjoining undertaker rooms.

"I know, I feel it, too. As I told you, things are getting a little out of hands lately."

"Cheryl has visions."

"Doesn't surprise me at all. She told me she hears things."

But Dorothea shook her head. "It is more than that. She has been inside the Bird Cage Theatre. The girl fainted there and had severe visions during more than one visit. The last one scared the wits out of me."

"Why is that? What has she seen?"

"Well, it is hard to explain. It seems as if she is time traveling. She claims she is in another time when these fitful dreams, as she calls them, bother her. To make the story short, she experienced how Mae lost her Russian Bill but not only that," Dorothea added with a shaky voice. She quickly took a few sips of the steaming coffee trying hard to calm down. Nora got up and refilled her friend's cup. She returned the pot on the coffeemaker and padded Dorothea's hand. "What else? Tell me, I need to know if I want to judge the situation right."

"Cheryl remembered every detail of the vision. She was very shaken up over it. It looks like Mae had committed suicide inside the Bird Cage but not only that. She cursed Hutchinson and touched him with her own blood before she passed away. She damned him into being a prisoner in that old brothel."

Nora grew pale. "Sweet Jesus, that explains a lot. Do you know what that means?"

Dorothea shook her head.

Nora stared toward the front door but seemed lost in thought. Her forehead was wrinkled in a frown and her eyebrows pulled together.

"This is worse than I ever imagined," she whispered.

"What do you mean?" Dorothea wanted to know.

"Well, the problem is that a curse cannot easily be broken. Sometimes spirits act as if to re-create the original situation which led to damnation. An evil spirit, and I do strongly believe that Hutchinson is such a devilish one, might try to lure the once involved back to where it all started. Either he wants to break the curse or he wants to capture Mae in the same hell he is stuck in."

"Oh, Lord in heaven, you think he wants to keep Cheryl inside the Bird Cage Theatre?" Dorothea trembled and her eyes were huge with fear.

Nora shook her head. "Not Cheryl but Mae. He does not understand that we are not in the 1880s anymore. The only thing which has protected her from harm so far is Russian Bill. Love is stronger than evil. But God only knows how long he can save her. He yearns for her and calls her back to that dang brothel just as Hutchinson does but for a different reason. He knows she should not return, but is Bill strong enough to sacrifice his longing and love for the sake to safe her?"

"What can we do? Should we encourage Cheryl to return to California?"

Nora nodded. "She needs to leave, Dorothea. Cheryl is in grave danger. I am not the kind of person to sugarcoat things, and I swear this can develop into a life-threatening situation within the blink of an eye."

Dorothea got up. "Thank you for your honesty and concern, Nora. I will talk to Bert right away about this."

Nora hugged the museum manager and turned toward the first visitor of the day.

When Dorothea returned to the Courthouse Museum, she pulled Bert aside and filled him in with what Nora had told her. Her husband's face looked ashen.

"Wow, this is a tricky situation," he said. "It is Cheryl's decision if she wants to leave or not. We cannot fire her, plus don't forget, the Arizona State Park management has a say in this as well. Unless we inform the board of directors of some wrongdoing, they would never fire Cheryl since she is on a study internship. Cheryl has done nothing wrong, and I don't want to damage her reputation or mess up future job opportunities for her by making up some fake accusations. To be honest, I have grown very fond of her and would hate to see her leave."

Dorothea looked utterly sad at that moment. "I will miss her terribly, but I fear for her, Bert." Despite their sadness about having to say goodbye sooner than expected, they both agreed to suggest an earlier departure from Tombstone to Cheryl.

CHAPTER 28

CHERYL MUST LEAVE

The following day Cheryl showed up paler than ever at work. But there was a smile on her face, and her eyes were shining despite being red and bloodshot. Obviously, she had not slept much but did not seem to be tired. She was rather exhilarated as if something exciting had happened to her. However, when Dorothea asked about it, Cheryl avoided answering and claimed she had to get things ready in the ticket booth.

Bert looked at their employee, a confused expression on his face. Later he asked if Dorothea knew why their trainee was so high-spirited today. Dorothea shrugged her shoulder. "I have no clue, but it seems weird."

"Do you think she takes drugs?" Bert asked.

"I don't think so," Dorothea said. "She takes too much care of her body, eats healthy food and such."

At closing time, Bert called Cheryl over to the side exit as he got ready for a last patrol walk of the courtyard before locking the place up. Bert's face was stern when he spoke to the young woman. "Cheryl, you know we've taken a liking to you. I hope you know you can talk with us any time in case something is bothering you."

She tried to avoid his gaze when she answered.

"One thing is sure—you've got a spooky little town here." It should have sounded like a joke, but Bert hadn't missed the tremble in her voice.

"Do you remember when I told you that Tombstone speaks to some people in dramatic ways?"

"Yeah, I remember."

He touched her shoulder lightly. Her skin was cold despite the warm evening sun. "Sometimes that can be dangerous. Not every spirit in this town is a good one. This is not some sort of fancy California game, Cheryl. If you underestimate the dark side of Tombstone, you may be in more danger than you could ever imagine."

Cheryl stared at him and was about to turn away, trying to shrug him off. But when she looked over his shoulder, she saw a man dangling on the rope on one of the gallows. His eyes were empty sockets, and his rotting, black tongue hung out of his mouth.

She felt nauseous and looked into Bert's face, interpreting his expression as a knowing one. *Oh my God, he knows what I see,* she thought. He must have seen the horrifying image himself. *Sweet Mother Mary, am I losing my mind?*

Bert held her tight while she wept like a small child, leaning against his shoulder. When they walked back into the Courthouse, he called his wife. "Cheryl should stay overnight at our house." Dorothea saw that her friend was crying. "What happened? Why are you crying?"

Cheryl didn't answer. "The gallows," Bert said. It was enough of an explanation for Dorothea.

"You will stay with us. We will pick up a bag with a few things, and you will sleep at our house tonight. There is no way we will leave you alone tonight," Dorothea announced in a matter-of-fact voice.

The two McEntires were extremely kind and generous people, and they did their best to make Cheryl feel comfortable and welcome in their house. Cheryl ended up staying not only one but for three nights. But on the fourth day she told them she would return to her house.

"It isn't my kind of thing to be a burden to anybody. I think it is about time you have the privacy of your home to yourself again." Dorothea tried to object, but Cheryl motioned her to hear her out.

"I haven't had any nightmares the past three nights, and no spirits have bothered me. It might have to do with the sage you burned every evening or simply because I was protected by your wonderful friendship. I reckon chances are that the entire mess is over."

"You can always stay here as our guest, my dear. We are here for you. Bert and I care for you, Cheryl."

Bert drove her back to Crazy Anne's house. For a moment Cheryl remembered how he had brought her here on her arrival day in Tombstone. It seemed like years ago. So much had happened since that day.

Cheryl entered the quiet house on the fourth day of her absence and decided to go to bed early. She wasn't hungry and turned in right after a shower. Despite being under the covers, she felt cold and shivered. But she was too tired to get back up and turn the heater on. Instead, Cheryl pulled the covers all the way up to her chin. However, it seemed the temperature in the room dropped further. "All right, get out of bed and turn the dang heater on before you freeze your buns off," she scolded herself. Cheryl turned and switched on the antique nightstand lamp. As the soft yellow light illuminated the room, a scream escaped Cheryl's lips.

A young woman in a burgundy bustle dress looked down at her. Her face bore a sad expression. Cheryl was about to jump out of bed but didn't dare move. *Is this Crazy Anne?* she wondered. But no, she somehow looked younger. It took Cheryl a few seconds, but thanks to the long, coppery hair, she recognized the stranger.

"My God, have mercy! You're Lizette, aren't you?" Cheryl whispered. The woman smiled at her.

"Good evening, Mae. It's good to see you back. He's so happy, Russian Bill is." The woman's voice sounded like that of a child.

Cheryl shook her head and covered her ears with her hands. "Stop this. I don't want to hear any more of this madness. My name is Cheryl. I am not Mae, and you do not exist. All of this crazy balderdash is not happening. I will return to California soon, and I will have a good life there. Leave me alone for Christ's sake."

But Lizette simply shook her head.

"He stood by his promise and came back. Russian Bill has waited for your return to the Bird Cage all these years. Every single night, Mae! We all have waited for you. When you cursed Hutchinson that fateful night and killed yourself, you didn't only force him into damnation but eventually chained your own soul to the building, same as ours."

Lizette raised her hands in a helpless gesture. Only then did Cheryl see the scars on Lizette's wrists and remembered what she read about the Flying Nymph committing suicide.

Lizette smiled at her, and the fact that Cheryl saw the rose pattern of the wallpaper through ghost's appearance made her skin crawl with goosebumps. She heard her voice loud and clear in her head, although she tried to block it off with her hands.

"The Bird Cage is our home, Mae! Russian Bill is your man. It is time for you to return. We are all waiting for you."

Cheryl stared at the woman, but before she could protest,

the image faded away. She shook her head and rubbed her eyes. Nobody but she was in the room. Cheryl hadn't been aware that she held her breath, and she exhaled it with a shiver. "Boy, oh boy, I think you need to see a shrink," she whispered into the empty bedroom. Just as she was convinced that her fantasy had played a trick on her and that she had not really seen Lizette, a light breeze brushed her cheek. The window and door to the adjoining bathroom were closed. With horror, Cheryl stared at the tiny black feather that danced through the air before it softly landed next to her hand on the bed cover. The scared student recalled having seen black feathers sewn to the sleeves of Lizette's dress.

Cheryl sobbed and hid under the covers, not daring to get out of bed. She lay there, crying for hours, feeling helpless like a child. Cheryl didn't know how to escape this sheer madness that had taken over her life. She was afraid she was about to lose her mind.

CHAPTER 29

DECIDING TO LEAVE

When Cheryl woke, she felt as if a truck had run over her. She made some strong coffee and sat on the porch steps, the hot cup in her ice-cold hands. The sun was rising but its warmth failed to calm the chills she felt inside.

What was she going to do? *I need to get out of here. If I stay, I am losing it.* By now she seriously considered leaving town. The entire story and haunted scene in Tombstone were way too much for her to bear. *I must talk to Dorothea and Bert. I am sure they will be utterly disappointed in me if I tell them I want to leave my assigned job much earlier, but I cannot take this anymore.*

Feeling torn and guilty, the devastated woman could not bring herself to openly admit that it wasn't only the McEntire couple she would feel sorry to leave. *God have mercy. I carry a man in my heart who has been dead over one hundred and thirty years. How in the world is that possible?*

Cheryl shook her head and walked back into the house to get ready for work. When she arrived at the Courthouse Museum, one look into Cheryl's haggard face was enough for Dorothea to understand that things had gotten worse the previous night. Her friend seemed distracted, and Dorothea saw the dark circles under her eyes. She held her tight for a moment. "Let's talk during lunch, dear. We will take you to a restaurant." Bert and Dorothea took Cheryl out to the O.K. Café and braced themselves for the conversation. "Cheryl, you are like a family member to us, and it saddens us deeply that you are suffering so bad since you work here in Tombstone," Bert said.

Dorothea took a sip of her iced tea as if to win time before she spoke. "Bert and I have been thinking about sending you home, back to California." When Cheryl started to protest, Bert hushed her.

"We are very happy with your work, and we truly love you, almost like a daughter. But we are very scared for your safety. Somehow, you seem to trigger much more paranormal action here than anybody else has before you. There is something about you that the spirits seek, and we fear that we don't have enough power to protect you, even with Nora's help. We know that mental and even physical harm can be done by events like the ones you are experiencing lately and would never forgive ourselves if anything happened to you."

Dorothea looked at Cheryl, tears in her eyes.

"We'll take care of your flight arrangements and make sure that the Arizona State Parks Board receives a proper explanation about your leaving earlier than scheduled. We will also make sure that you get the full acknowledgement for your term here to avoid that your leaving ahead of finishing day would disqualify you from further studies."

Cheryl felt a lump in her throat. She never thought this would happen and didn't really want to leave Tombstone. She had gotten used to the town, its old buildings, and the eccentric people and rowdy saloons but also knew that Bert was right about her being in some sort of danger.

With tears pooling in her eyes and with a heavy heart, she

finally agreed to take a direct flight to L.A. the coming weekend. She needed a few days to arrange accommodation in California as her apartment was rented out to a fellow student for at least another two months. Cheryl also wanted to finish her essay about the soiled doves of Tombstones silver rush as long as she had Dorothea's books with her and felt the atmosphere of the streets where they roamed in the old days. For some reason it felt wrong to write down their story in hectic, modern Los Angeles. The student didn't have the feeling that she would achieve a good result for her studies if she wrote her essay in a city that was as far from the history of the mining camp shady ladies as Beverly Hills was from the moon.

After lunch and finishing her work of the day at the museum, she returned to Crazy Anne's historic house in the early evening. She went to bed less than an hour after sunset and swallowed a pill to guarantee deep sleep. Cheryl didn't want any more of those fitful dreams or visions of ghosts. All she wanted was to be at peace, as she felt emotionally drained. Sleep, undisturbed sleep, was all she wished for.

The pharmaceutical product did its work, and her sleep was dreamless for nine hours straight without waking. However, she was not alone in the room. Russian Bill sat next to her and stroked her hair. His body left no imprint on the bed sheets. He looked sad, then he vanished and with him the whiff of cherry tobacco.

It was the darkest hour before dawn. The Bird Cage Theatre lay in shadows except for the emergency exit lights. Hutchinson's rude voice boomed through the crowded bar area as he mocked Russian Bill.

"Your little filly won't come back to you it seems. Looks like I am not the only one to get punished by her. So, I am the one who wins after all."

The handsome William Tattenbaum stared at his opponent

through gray-blue, steely eyes. Hutchinson's face was a mask of pure hatred. When he turned around, his features showed the print of a slender hand on his left cheek.

The marks were the same color of crimson as the big stain spreading on the floor in front of the bar. It was there, reappearing again and again like it had had so many nights since 1882, but none of the museum employees ever saw it as it faded away into the past every morning long before they unlocked the doors to the museum.

CHAPTER 30

PREPARING TO SAY GOODBYE

The date of the flight back to California was set, and Cheryl had only another three days remaining in Tombstone. She walked along Allen Street to visit Nora one more time and to thank her for her help. The shop owner stood behind her counter filling out an order sheet when Cheryl walked into the store.

"Hey, girl, what are you up to?" Nora smiled.

Cheryl shrugged her shoulders. "Nothing much. To be honest, I came to say goodbye. I'm leaving town day after tomorrow."

Nora murmured, "You're afraid, aren't you?"

"Yes, or let's say, I need to have a good night's rest without seeing all this crazy stuff."

Nora was no fool. Although Cheryl tried to pretend to make things humorous, it was apparent she was terrified. She trembled and looked utterly pale. Nora opened one of the glass displays, bringing out a small pendant with a beautiful light blue crystal which reminded Cheryl of an aquamarine. Nora gently placed it into Cheryl's hand.

"This will protect you. Wear it as long as you are here, or even better, wear it all the time. It's my farewell gift to you. I think you made the right decision to leave this town."

Surprised by the gift, Cheryl put the small item in her hand. Then she pulled the thin leather cord over her head. The pendant seemed warm on her chest despite the fact that it was a cool crystal. She thanked Nora and hugged her intensely.

"One day, I will visit you again." Then she swallowed hard and turned around to leave.

The older woman's gaze followed her out the door. "I hope and pray you never come back, girl!" she whispered.

Nora worried that it might be too late for Cheryl to save herself and was very concerned about the increased activity in the old morgue during the past few days. For the first time, and despite being certain that the spirits would not harm Nora, she felt insecure about running the paranormal investigation tours. She knew that there was a thin line between doing it for touristy fun or getting herself into severe danger.

The following day Cheryl decided to pay one last visit to the haunted theatre. Most of her stuff was packed for the next day's flight, and she was off work before going to her farewell dinner with Bert and Dorothea.

Returning to the loud and bustling city of L.A. was not something to look forward to. Cheryl wasn't the same person she was when she first set foot in this Western frontier town many weeks ago. She had seen and experienced things that changed her life.

It was mystifying that she felt so comfortable in the historic Bird Cage, but at the same time knew she would feel out of place in L.A. the next day. What was happening to her?

Cheryl bought a ticket at the entrance to the museum. She didn't know the lady on duty and didn't mind paying. She saw a dark stain on the floor in front of the bar. *Maybe it is only a shadow from the bright daylight seeping through the open door? Maybe I see these things because my imagination is in overdrive?*

Fortunately, the place wasn't busy as she had come at a late hour. Most tourists were either on their way out of town or in one of the restaurants and saloons for an early dinner. Generally, during the last two hours of the workday neither stores nor museums were crowded. Especially during weekdays, the town wasn't too busy after 4:30 p.m.

When Cheryl entered the gloomy back room, she was alone with the big stage and the cribs below the ceiling. It reminded her of the first visit when no one else had been around and Cheryl felt as if she was coming home. She immediately walked to the poker booth next to the stage. She wasn't surprised to see a cigar which lay burning in a small glass ashtray. The faint aroma of cherry tobacco tickled her nose.

"Bill!" she called, but there was no answer. She walked behind the stage and avoided eye contact with the funeral hearse. It still made her uneasy to look at it. The wooden stairs creaked as she took them down to the basement bordello. The sound seemed unnaturally loud. When the lone visitor reached the first chamber, she felt the gentle touch of a breeze caressing her neckline. She closed her eyes as if to enjoy a tender lover's touch.

The voice whispered into her ear. "Why are you leaving me, Mae? I kept my promise like I told you I would. Why do you betray my love?"

Cheryl didn't know what to say. Tears rolled down her ashen cheeks as she turned her head toward the shadow next to her.

"It's not possible. You are in your world, the dark world, and I live in a different time. I want to be with you, but I can't even touch you. If I stay here, I'll lose my mind. I will be yearning for you without hope, and I fear Hutchinson. There is no other way."

Weeping bitterly and blinded by her tears, she stumbled into the next room and left the museum through the gift shop. But this time the ghost of Russian Bill didn't follow.

Two hours later Cheryl sat at the table of the Longhorn Restaurant with Bert and Dorothea. The food was delicious, but she had lost her appetite. To say goodbye to the old brothel and Russian Bill had been devastating and heartbreaking.

The friendly couple tried their best to cheer their guest up and to involve Cheryl in bubbling small talk about God and the whole world, but somehow the woman seated across from them couldn't pull herself out of her gloomy mood. "I know it was hard for you to say goodbye to the Bird Cage Theatre today but it is better this way, believe me, my dear," Dorothea said while she patted Cheryl's hand. Shortly after eight o'clock, Cheryl excused herself, fibbing that she still had some packing to do.

She just wanted to be alone. Bert dropped her off at the charming historic house Cheryl had called home during the past three months and gave her one of his bear hugs.

"Sleep well, little L.A. cowgirl," he whispered. "Don't be sad, we will always be your friends, and hey, we might come to see you in Los Angeles next spring."

Cheryl hugged him back and thanked him for the nice evening and the ride. Dorothea remained seated in the car. She was depressed to have to say goodbye to the girl she got to love like a daughter.

Bert and Dorothea had promised to pick her up around noon the next day for the airport transfer to Tucson.

By the time Cheryl had showered it was past 9.30 p.m., and she sat in her rocking chair on the porch, wrapped in a warm sweater and wearing an old, faded denim. Loneliness held her heart in its cold grip. She wasn't aware of the fact that she was waiting for him, sniffing the night air for the familiar smell of cherry cigar smoke like a puppy. But this time Russian Bill didn't appear or talk to her.

He must feel betrayed, Cheryl thought. Starting to feel cold, she got up and went inside the house. In bed, she snuggled under the cozy covers recalling the past crazy weeks in Tombstone. All of the weird things that had happened seemed so unreal.

Oh, how much I miss him. Now she knew why she had waited for her Prince Charming, why it had to be a long-haired fellow with gray eyes. My subconscious must have remembered Russian Bill's handsome features and long wavy hair all these years. Maybe her soul was still longing for the love of her life, of a time gone by so long ago. Cheryl had accepted the thought that she was the re-incarnated Mae without even being aware of it. She no longer fought against the truth. But how should she continue living her life as Cheryl Roberts now?

Feeling depressed she closed her eyes, trying to get some sleep while wishing more than anything that she could see him and hear Russian Bill one last time before leaving Arizona the following day.

Leaving—never in her life had that word sounded so cruel, so unbearable. She had waited in vain for him, and she had lost it all. *I can't recall ever feeling so lonely in my entire life*, she thought and wiped away a salty tear rolling down her right cheek.

CHAPTER 31

A FATAL DECISION

*I*t was past midnight. The building was empty. A shadow sat in the poker booth next to the stage. The day's tourists had left, and the spirits of the ladies and gentlemen invisible to most human beings remained silent that night.

They shared one emotion in common, the grief over a lost life, a fortune gone, and the loss of love. They were hell-bound and caught in the building that had become their destiny for eternity.

Russian Bill shuffled the cards, his cigar untouched in the crystal ashtray. Helplessly his soul had to accept the fact that he had no way to reach the woman that once had been the love of his short life. The handsome gambler had failed to hold her back in Tombstone. He put the cards onto the velvet covered, old table, face down. He selected one card and held it up. It was the queen of hearts. "I waited a hundred and thirty-six years for her. In vain, all in vain. This wound will never close. I am cursed to feel the loneliness of having lost her love forever," he whispered.

He vanished. The only thing left was the queen of hearts next to the ashtray with the gleaming cigar in it.

Cheryl flipped through the pages of the *Soiled Doves of the West* book. Sleep simply would not come. She looked at the photos of long forgotten times. Women in daring clothes captured in their most private moments lingered in tempting poses.

The picture of Lizette in the middle of the book was haunting. What a beautiful woman she had been, but how tragically her life had ended. Yet Cheryl envied her over the fact that Lizette had known Mae and Russian Bill, Crazy Anne, and Curly Bill in person, and even more so, Lizette was still able to be with them. *I, the spoiled California girl, am not as lucky,* she thought. No, she had to return to a world that meant nothing to her anymore. Jealousy rushed through her like a burning flame. As she stared at the sepia-colored portrait of Lizette with her gorgeous long hair, which Cheryl knew once had the color of copper, a thought crossed her mind.

By God, the solution to all her problems had been right there, reachable all this time. *There is indeed a way to turn back time. I just didn't see it, being too busy with denying the plain facts.* Her ability to observe a problem from every angle must have been lost for a while.

She chuckled at herself. Now she knew what she had to do. There was a way out of this misery.

Cheryl eagerly jumped out of bed and stood in front of the antique dressing mirror wearing only her underwear. Calmly she pinned up her hair with two old-fashioned combs she had bought in one of the shops a few days back.

She turned around and opened the zipper of her red suitcase. Just like the second piece of luggage on the floor, it was packed to the limit. She'd surely have to pay extra for excess weight but didn't mind. "Didn't have that kind of problem during old stagecoach times I guess," Cheryl laughed hysterically to the empty room.

On top of her clothes the green bustle dress lay neatly folded. With an almost tender caress she touched the skirt and jacket that Dorothea had given her. The shimmering material rustled softly as she unpacked it from her luggage, the luggage of a different time and a different life.

The young woman stepped into the skirt. It fell billowing around her ankles but was a bit loose. She hadn't been aware how much weight she'd lost the past few days. It didn't matter.

After putting on her shoes she slipped into the embroidered jacket with its tiny silk-covered buttons. Although she looked gorgeous, the reflection in the mirror looked way thinner and paler than upon arrival in Tombstone.

Cheryl smoothed the lace collar around her neck tenderly. Then she put on an antique-looking choker with matching earrings. She was pleased with what she saw in the mirror and smiled. *How astonishing. I almost look like the woman I saw in the dressing mirror of the first chamber at the Bird Cage.* "Why does it surprise you? Aren't you Mae?" she whispered and felt a chill up and down her spine.

Cheryl's cell phone lay next to her purse on the bedside table. Something seemed to be caught between her breasts, and she pulled on the thin leather cord which held the crystal Nora had given her. She reached for the pendant and slid the leather string carefully over her head. Then she placed it tenderly next to her phone. It had been nice of Nora to give it to her, but she wouldn't need it tonight, and she would have no use for modern communication techniques where she was going either.

The beautifully clad lady stepped out of the house and left the property through the garden gate in the middle of the night. She set one foot in front of the other, listening to each hollow clack caused by her heels, but her pace didn't lack confidence even though it was dark.

Cheryl chose the back road behind Allen Street so she wouldn't run into anybody, but her worries were in vain. No one was on the street. It was well past midnight, and as usual on a weekday, the town was deserted.

There was a chill in the late-night air, but Cheryl didn't feel it. The cold wind went through the fabric of her jacket, but it didn't bother her. All she could think of were Russian Bill's blue-gray eyes and the love shining in them.

Walking confidently, she passed the area that had been Tombstone's famous red-light district in the 1880s. Cheryl looked gorgeous in her dress with her dark hair pinned up, almost like an entirely different woman. The way she looked she could have stepped out of a Hollywood Western production. A gentle smile lit up her face. A few stubborn curls of her hair had freed themselves from the combs and caressed her cheeks and neckline.

Finally, she arrived at the historic Bird Cage Theatre. The building lay in complete darkness. The only light source came from a streetlight on the opposite corner. It was nearly 1:00 a.m. on October 28.

Cheryl stood in front of the main door and took a deep breath. What she didn't know was that over one hundred and thirty-six years ago on the very same date a dark-haired woman stormed into the notorious premises through that very door while she was screaming furiously.

A soft breeze ruffled Cheryl's long bustle skirt. She turned and took a last glance at the cars parked close by, a last peek at the souvenir shops and saloons. And then she finally saw them, the shadows of townsfolk long gone. They were walking along the boardwalk, smiling at her. Prospectors and cowboys bowed their heads in a respectful greeting. She did not fear them any longer.

Cheryl Roberts turned back to the door and gently pushed against it, not at all surprised that it swung open for her. She had been certain that the theatre would welcome her back home. As Cheryl stepped through the front door, she left the modern world behind, but it did not bother her at all as she was where she belonged. There was no feeling of loss. She was Mae Davenport. Cheryl Roberts was not important anymore. All that counted was Russian Bill and a carnival dancer named Mae and their unwavering love for each other.

The theatre was filled with the loud roar of the crowd and the piano playing polka from the Old World. The men at the bar toasted her, their glasses filled with ember-colored whiskey. The booth next to the stage was empty. Nobody shuffled the cards there, but Cheryl didn't worry about it. She knew he was waiting for her in the very same room where they had made love the first time. All she had to do was walk downstairs. With a knowing smile, the beautiful woman stepped behind the stage and was on her way to the basement.

CHAPTER 32

DISCOVERY

$\mathcal{T}$he next morning the museum employee named Heather opened the front door to the Bird Cage Theatre. As so often the lock didn't work well.

"Need to tell the owner to do something about that stupid locking system. Sooner or later, I'll break the key, and then he'll raise hell over it, putting the blame on me as usual. Wonder if it was even locked right last night," she mumbled while rattling impatiently at the door handle.

Heather didn't bother to write a note about it in the daily report but simply punched a short message to the owner into her cell phone.

"Praise modern electronics," she said and got the roll of blue-colored admission tickets ready for the day.

Heather followed her usual routine. Besides getting the cash register ready, she had to do a control walk through the entire double story building, checking if everything was okay.

"Man, I am sure I will run out of change before lunch time." She cussed when she counted the notes and coins. "Well, better do my rounds and make sure all doors inside are unlocked for the tourists. Hope we get a decent number of groups today. The low tips suck lately," she mumbled. Her friends made fun of Heather over her tendency to talk to herself in the museum, but she knew better. It was rather comforting to hear her own voice and distracted her from the sounds and whispers she often heard inside the structure.

All doors had to be open except those of the brothel chambers, of course. They remained locked the entire year.

Heather was sure she had to restock the gift store this morning. The weekend was just around the corner, and as far as she remembered, they had to refill some of the postcards. Surely a book or two was sold out as well, but some of them should still be in stock in boxes in the tiny storage room behind the bar.

As Heather walked downstairs, the odd feeling that something was different that day made her nervous. Not that she would have been astonished if things had been moved around. Tourists had funny ideas from time to time, and Heather knew that weird incidents happened in the place during the night as well.

Not every night, but this was said to be a haunted building. Heather didn't question it anymore as she had seen her share of strange things inside this place with its infamous reputation.

When she arrived at the bottom of the stairs, she froze in her tracks, staring in shock at the open door of the first chamber.

"Now who in this god-forsaken town would dare to break open the locked door of a museum?" she swore.

"I don't believe it. How am I going to explain this to the big boss? By God, I hope nothing has been stolen or damaged. It would get me fired in the blink of an eye!"

Heather was furious. The break-in must have happened during the evening shift. She had told the owner of the museum right away that the new girl was not the right one for the job.

Heather had judged her as not very reliable right from the start and told him so.

"Weed smoking punk," she muttered. She hoped that nothing had been violated in the historic prostitution chamber and hesitantly took a step forward. But when she looked at the door frame, she realized that the lock wasn't broken. It appeared as if it had been simply unlocked. None of the employees held keys for the three basement chambers. They were in a safe at the owner's house.

"I'll be darned. Has he opened it himself?" she whispered.

She reluctantly stepped forward and caught a whiff of a pleasant tobacco smell. Heather gazed into the small, gloomy room. At first, she didn't understand what she saw.

It took her a few seconds to realize what was wrong in that room. When the scene finally hit home, she screamed and could barely stop. Her terrified voice echoed from the cool adobe walls. She turned and scrabbled frantically upstairs holding onto the old banister railing.

The McEntires drove to the Victorian house a few minutes before ten. They had come up with the idea of pampering Cheryl with a last one of Carmen's incredible breakfasts at the O.K. Café. The couple wanted to spend as much of the remaining time with their California friend as possible.

Bert and Dorothea understood each other without words after so many years of marriage and knew how much they would miss Cheryl once her flight back to Los Angeles departed from Tucson. The couple had grown fond of the young woman and wished she didn't have to leave.

When they parked their car in front of Crazy Anne's house, they heard the siren of the sheriff's car whining along Fremont Street followed by an ambulance only moments later.

"What's the commotion all about?" Bert wondered, but Dorothea shrugged her shoulders.

"Will probably not take too long before we hear it through the grapevine. Maybe another drunk who fell down the stairs of his trailer," she added and knocked at the door, but Cheryl didn't open it.

Dorothea frowned. "Hm, maybe she is still asleep. After all, she hasn't been getting the rest she urgently needs. I am sure she is terribly exhausted."

"Probably true," Bert said. "Cannot blame her for oversleeping a bit. We still have enough time to have breakfast. Her flight won't leave until the late afternoon anyway."

After giving another knock at the door, the couple waited in vain for their friend to open. So, Dorothea dialed Cheryl's mobile phone, trying to reach her.

"Maybe she's out already walking through town on a last-minute hunt for souvenirs for her L.A. friends," Bert suggested.

The phone rang, but no one answered. Just when she was about to disconnect the call, Bert's wife heard a phone ringing inside the house which sounded like Cheryl's. She looked at Bert. He started to knock at the front door again, harder this time. No answer.

Meanwhile a third car with sirens blaring raced along Freemont Street. A Tucson police car.

"What in the world?" Bert McEntire walked toward the street corner of Tough Nut Street and Allen Street and looked in the direction where the noise came from. His face showed a worried expression when he realized that all the rescue forces had parked their vehicles in front of the famous historic theatre across from the Silver Nugget Hotel and Mercantile. A crowd of locals had gathered already, and the parked cars of the authorities still had their blue and red lights flashing.

"I wonder if they have an emergency with a tourist in the museum. What a mess to have that kind of trouble barely an hour after opening. Not the best way to start the day," Bert mumbled.

He walked back to the house where his wife still waited for Cheryl to open the front door. She looked at him, then at the phone in her hand still ringing after she dialed Cheryl's number for the fifth time without getting an answer. Dorothea frowned, glanced up toward the other end of Allen Street, and all color drained from her worried face.

"My God, the Bird Cage." Dorothea turned and took off at a rapid pace toward the old adobe building up the street.

Her husband called after her. "Hey woman, where are you going? What in the world is wrong?"

But she didn't pay any attention to him. "Sweet Jesus, let me be wrong about this," she prayed loudly while walking along the street as fast as she could, panting hard.

Her husband followed but could barely keep up with her. "Dorothea, what's the matter?"

"I think I know where she is, but I hope I am wrong," she called back over her shoulder never stopping her fast stride. By the time they passed Big Nose Kate's Saloon, they saw the rescue teams and started to run along the boardwalk, their sneakers hitting the wooden blanks with dull thuds.

When they arrived at the historical structure, they saw Heather leaning against the shoulders of a policeman. She was sobbing hard, her mascara leaving black traces on her face.

The onlookers were trying their best to get the perfect view while pointing their cell phones toward the entrance. Everybody wanted to get the best shot of whatever was happening inside, and Bert's face showed the dismay over witnessing the sensationism.

A paramedic wheeled a gurney into the museum. A hush went through the crowd. "Somebody must have been hurt in there," a lady in shorts and pink flip flops speculated.

Heather turned away from the paramedics. That was when she saw the McEntire couple and reached out her hand.

"I am so sorry Dorothea. I don't know how this could have happened."

Meanwhile, a worried looking Nora walked out of the Paranormal Sisters Shop toward them. Bert looked at her questioningly, but Nora shrugged her shoulders. "I have no clue what's going on in there." Heather stared at Dorothea trying to get her sobbing under control.

"What do you mean with you are sorry? Sorry for what?" Dorothea wanted to know.

Heather cried hysterically, and nobody understood what she was saying until a single word turned Dorothea's blood to ice. "Cheryl."

Bert tried to hold back his wife, but she slipped out of her jacket and ran into the museum frantically calling the name of her friend over and over again. Nora covered her face with her hands. She looked white as a bed sheet, and fear showed in her eyes.

The sheriff tried to restrain Dorothea, but despite her age, she was fast like a cat. Nobody was capable of preventing her from entering the museum.

She stood in the gloomy main theatre room for a few seconds trying to adjust her eyes to the semi darkness, but then she heard the noises coming from the downstairs area, and Dorothea crossed the main museum room as fast as her feet would carry her.

"Downstairs. The voices come from the poker room," she whispered as if to encourage herself. When she arrived at the base of the stairs, the entire basement was extremely crowded with people. Powerful spotlights almost blinded her, and she held her hand over her eyes shielding them against the glare.

When her eyes adjusted to the bright lights which seemed so

out of place in this building, she realized that the door to the first chamber of the fallen angels stood wide open. Male voices were all around her, but there was something else. She felt some sort of energy, like humming electricity.

Dorothea McEntire didn't know how to walk toward the door. She hesitated as the gurney blocked her step. It was positioned in front of the banister railing that divided the poker area from the pass way along the three chambers. The basement was too cramped with furniture and artifacts to handle the medical equipment. The rescue team members literally stood on each other's toes.

"Oh, God, no." Cheryl's friend didn't want to walk any closer, fearing what might be ahead. She turned away but caught a glimpse of a shimmering green skirt and froze.

"That looks like the material of my dress. For the mercy of God, don't let it be Cheryl in there." She stifled a cry as she set one foot in front of the other. The historic chamber pulled her closer, like a magnet, and after a few hesitant steps the frightened woman stood in the doorway.

The sheriff who had followed wanted to pull Dorothea back to lead her out of the building, but it was too late. She had seen what she wasn't supposed to witness.

Cheryl Roberts lay on the small antique bed. She wore Dorothea's gifted bustle dress. A few strands of hair covered part of her forehead and right cheek. Her face was the color of pale wax, and her lips were blue, yet she looked incredibly beautiful. The lips had parted in a petite smile showing pearly white teeth. Her left arm hung beside the bed, limp. Her right hand clutched what looked like a small, brown glass bottle. She almost looked like a Victorian doll from a time long forgotten and fit into the room in an eerie way unlike all the modern-day people who rather appeared as intruders.

"Cheryl?" Dorothea called her friend's name. Against her

better judgement, she hoped that Cheryl would open her eyes. "What in the world is she doing here? Cheryl, girl, open your eyes for me, please." Dorothea started to sob as she stared at the unmoving woman on the bed.

One of the paramedics kneeled in front of her checking for vital signs. After what seemed like an eternity to Dorothea, he slowly got up and shook his head.

"She's dead," he announced gravely. "There's nothing we can do."

Dorothea broke down. "That's not possible. How can she be dead, and how in the world did she get into the Bird Cage all by herself? The place is barely open for an hour. Heather must have seen what happened. Who would want to harm her?" Dorothea yelled at the young man. "Try to revive her, for Christ's sake. Don't just stand there, do something."

The heavy-set man stood in the middle of the crib room and stared at the ground, not knowing what to say. Then he pointed at Cheryl. He raised his hands in a helpless gesture.

"She must've been dead for at least five to seven hours. There's no point trying to bring her back, you understand?"

No, Cheryl's friend did not understand any of this. "How can this be? How can Cheryl be gone?" she whispered as tears rolled down her weathered cheeks.

The sheriff pointed to the brown bottle.

"What is that? Let me see it."

The paramedic used a gloved hand to gently remove the glass bottle from Cheryl's cold fingers which had turned stiff already. Fortunately, the glass was smooth enough to free it from her cramped cold hand so he didn't have to break her slender fingers. He looked at the bottle in disbelief.

"I'll be darned!"

"What is it?" the sheriff asked impatiently. The other fellow looked at the officer while he sniffed the neck of the bottle. "The label says laudanum in handwriting! It's freaking laudanum, the stuff that knocked out many of the soiled doves in the old days. It looks like an original bottle to me. Definitely smells like laudanum. Where in the world did she get that?"

Everybody looked rather confused except for Dorothea. She understood perfectly. Sobbing, she walked out of the room. When she met Bert at the entrance, he held her close, not daring to ask his wife what she saw. She cried hard and finally told him it was Cheryl down there and that she was dead.

Bert couldn't believe his ears. "What are you saying, woman. I don't like to be fooled, Dorothea. We saw her only a few hours ago. This must be a mistake."

❧❧❧❧❧❧❧

HIS WIFE LOOKED at him through swollen eyes. Then she started to stammer and told him the truth. "She went to be with him, Bert! It was the only way to return to Russian Bill. May God forgive us! We should have known better. How could we underestimate the power of the evil side of Tombstone's past? We should have been aware that they wouldn't let her go. I'll never forgive myself."

Nora stood beside them. She covered her face with her hands. "I have failed. I knew how bad the spirits wanted her. We should have brought her to the airport days ago. Sweet Jesus, we could have avoided it."

Devastated, the McEntires and Nora left the scene while the onlookers still remained standing in front of the building waiting for the paramedics to return with the gurney. All the people knew was that someone died inside the Bird Cage Theatre.

The paramedics gently placed Cheryl's stiff body onto the gurney and covered her with a white sheet to protect her from tourist's curiosity. Everybody was shocked about the fact that someone took her life in the building with its haunted reputation. Nobody could prevent this tragedy from happening, but the sheriff made sure that nobody was taking unwanted pictures of the dead woman. It was a matter of dignity.

Back in the Victorian home of Crazy Anne, Cheryl's open suitcase waited for flight AA 302 to Los Angeles. But Cheryl would never return to that place and life.

CHAPTER 33

INVESTIGATION

The Tucson police conducted a thorough investigation over the following days. Although it was obvious that Cheryl's death was a suicide, her passing left a lot of unanswered questions, and this time the police was determined to look into the case from every possible angle. The authorities had been blamed for failure in finding out the truth in Lisa's case, and they didn't want to appear incapable to solve crimes when they occurred. Of course, Cheryl's suicide was not as much a mystery as Lisa's disappearance had been. But the question was how the woman got into the locked museum and how it was possible for her to lay hands on a bottle of an 1880s drug.

Meanwhile, Dorothea and Bert tried their best to reach Cheryl's relatives in California. They had no clue what they should tell them. How could they explain the suicide of a fun-loving young woman?

The owner of the famous brothel and theatre had to keep the place closed for the duration of the investigation. But not only that—he also had to provide access to every room including both bordello chambers, the small cellar at the end of the gambling area, and of course, the former bath and changing room of the gamblers in the basement, which had never been open to public since the late 1950s.

The forensic people felt uneasy when the third door was unlocked by Mister Bronley, the owner himself. He looked unusually pale and fiddled with his key ring. He turned an old looking key in the lock which snapped open with a loud *click*.

The officers hesitated to walk into the tiny room. Something seemed odd in there. When Bronley carefully opened the door after so many years, the air in it escaped with an angry hiss, or was it a voice? None of them was sure and looked at each other nervously. One of the forensics wondered why Bronley touched the door handle with his sleeve wrapped around his hand, but before he could even think about it, the sickening, sweet smell of decaying flesh escaped the room. The superior of the investigation specialists had been working with the police department for over three decades, and he immediately recognized the smell. He pulled back his shoulders and held his breath as if preparing himself for the worst.

When he walked through the door, he stood frozen in the gloomy twilight. He immediately raised his hand motioning his team not to enter the small, dark room. The man's face bore an expression of shock and disgust. The decaying corpse of a blond woman sat in an old-fashioned chair. A pile of silver coins lay on the ground next to her feet. She stared at him through empty eye sockets. Next to her lay the skeleton of another female on the dusty floor. A faded cape made of feathers partly covered her bones.

He tumbled backward and hollered for the leading police officer who was upstairs. When Officer McCain arrived in the basement, the other man pointed to the third door. "We have a severe problem, sir. This suicide has just turned into a major murder investigation."

"What the heck are you talking about?" McCain wanted to know. "I might be wrong, but chances are that I found the missing Lisa Callaghan. He stepped aside, and Officer McCain walked reluctantly into the tiny chamber.

"Sweet Jesus, what in the world has happened to her?" The leader of the forensic team shrugged his shoulders. "I don't know yet. Could have been a heart attack, since I don't see any obvious injuries, but after the student knocking her light out with laudanum, I wouldn't be surprised if we find more unpleasant surprises. Did you see the other skeleton on the floor? Those remains look at least over fifty years old, likely even much older. That cape looks antique and authentic. I will not be able to say what that person died from unless there is a skull damage. Question is, how for the sake of crazy Hannah did those folks get into a room which had been locked since 1956?"

"I swear to God, nobody had access to that very room since my parents bought the place," Bronley insisted. "The key was in our safe deposit back home all these years. We don't even have a spare. I don't understand how this is possible. Jesus, I am ruined when the public gets to know this." He turned around and panted as he walked upstairs. McCain pointed to one of his officers. "Follow him and make sure he understands that he has to stay in town in case we have questions. Oh, and ask him if he is all right. He looked a bit cheesy around his nose."

"Who wouldn't if authorities found three dead people in your business," the forensic pathologist mumbled.

The police turned the whole place upside down. The owner complained about the loss of business, but the lead detective made it clear that he would be lucky if the museum could stay open at all. The Tucson police department threatened to detain him if he didn't cooperate.

The media was all over the place questioning people in every shop along Allen Street and each saloon. After all, it wasn't only a suicide that took place in the famous museum, but there was also the rumor that evidence for murders had been found. Of course, all the *saloon experts* had to share their two cents with the media, and as usual, tall tales were told.

The crime lab in Tucson worked day and night for five days straight and issued the final report, which was only partly shared with the reporters because the authorities didn't want to jeopardize the investigations. To everybody's surprise, a fourth victim was mentioned in the documents. While searching the entire premises, a skull of a female had been found among the antique whiskey barrels and old furniture in the small vault cellar under the main stage. The skull had been there for over a hundred years, hidden behind the iron bars.

Two of the females' remains were dated as quite old, their deaths occurring between fifty to a hundred years back. Not so the passing of the blond woman in chamber number three. The body was identified as that of Lisa Callaghan who had been reported missing weeks before.

According to the medical examiner, Lisa's cause of death was most likely heart failure. However, nobody knew how she had gotten into that third tiny room that had been locked several decades. Her mouth had been open in a silent scream. Whatever scared her caused a cardiac arrest.

No explanation could be found for the coins lying on the ground around Lisa's feet. Experts proved they were authentic 1882 Morgan Dollars minted of pure Tombstone silver prospected during the town's silver rush.

The female skeleton wrapped in a cape lying next to Lisa had belonged to a woman who had been around thirty years of age when she died. The cause of death was not detectable anymore. The position of the bones on the floor suggested violence though. The remaining bones of the fourth person were never found. The form and edges of the skull suggested it had been another female.

Nobody could identify the two older skeletons, but Dorothea assumed they were the two missing women she had come across in her research. It was impossible to obtain DNA evidence to be certain of their identity. Too many years had passed since their death. They remained unnamed lost souls, and the cause of their deaths would always be a mystery.

As for Cheryl, she had committed suicide by drinking the contents of an original bottle of the frontier pain drug known as laudanum. The weird part was that not a single bottle of laudanum had ever been displayed in the museum. Unlike the old morgue, the Bird Cage Theatre had no original liquids on display, except for a few newer bottles of liquors on the bar for decoration in the front room. However, the toxicology report was consistent with the original formula from the late 1800s. Nobody had a clue where Cheryl got the bottle from, but Dorothea knew.

Cheryl's body was flown to her family in California. The funeral service would be held in Los Angeles. Bert shed a tear when the coroner drove off to the airport with Cheryl's body. "It should have been us dropping her off at the airport. She was not supposed to fly back in a dang casket," he sobbed.

Dorothea hugged her husband. "We will have a walk down for her on Allen Street, and we both know that she is not really gone. She just went to the other side of the gateway, Bert. She is home. Mae is back home."

CHAPTER 34

THE BIRD CAGE IS ALIVE

*T*he night was dark and cloudy with no souls on the road. The main tourist season and the annual events were over. It was much colder than a few weeks ago, and one of the rare Arizona rain showers turned the red colored dirt on Allen Street to slippery mud.

The old brothel and gambling house lay in complete darkness. To the modern outside world, the windows were like the dark eyes of a stranger staring down on the street and peering at the opposite buildings.

But inside, the smoke was thick, and the laughter and music equally loud.

Can-can dancers tempted their audience, showing their legs beneath their swirling skirts imported all the way from Paris in the Old World. The dancers' costumes revealed more than would have been appropriate among the town's so-called pure women.

The poker booth sat empty next to the stairs. No one shuffled a deck of cards there tonight. Downstairs the longest poker game of all frontier towns went on uninterrupted. Highest stakes of silver coins, mining deeds, and dollars exchanged hands. Some soiled doves provided whiskey refills to the gambling men, and some tried to lure the gamblers into the cribs upstairs, away from their deck of cards.

But all that didn't matter to the two lovers behind the first door. A beautiful woman with dark hair and huge brown eyes looked up at her handsome man while she caressed his bare torso. She knew every inch of his soft skin and marveled at it.

Mae Davenport held Russian Bill as tight as she could, his moves throwing her into a frenzy of passion. She cried out his name as her female lust swept her away. Mae had followed her Bill through the gateway into the past. She sacrificed her modern life for the one and only reason—to feel his promised love and to find herself in his arms again like she once had over one hundred thirty-six years earlier. This is where she belonged. The Bird Cage Theatre was her home and Russian Bill the love of her life for eternity.

$\wp\!\sim\!\wp\!\sim\!\wp\!\sim\!\wp\!\sim\!\wp\!\sim\!\wp$

OUTSIDE THE BUILDING and in the modern days, Tombstone entertained the visitors while the town was covered in the night's velvety darkness. The streetlights didn't reach the rear parking lot where Melissa always parked free of charge when coming to town to party, which was quite often the case.

"I drank too much of that dang tequila," Melissa mumbled, her speech slurred as she stumbled along the boardwalk.

She loved karaoke night at Doc Holliday's Saloon, and the guy running the equipment was kind of cute, at least after a few shots. She giggled for no reason at all. It was obvious she was drunk.

She dropped her car keys trying to unlock her old Ford pickup truck which was parked with its tail toward the Bird

Cage Theatre. She leaned against the driver's door and cussed like no decent woman would have ever done. Ignoring a hiccup, she bent down, nearly losing her balance on her high heels but managed to get hold of her key ring. As she fumbled with the keys, she heard his voice.

"A silver dollar should be enough for you, little bird."

Melissa turned but didn't see anybody. She shrugged her shoulders and tried to insert the key into the lock of the car door. "Wished I had a newer model where you just have to push a button to open the dang thing," she mumbled.

A sudden chilly breeze made her shiver, and the cold crawled along her shapely legs under the miniskirt she wore. Suddenly the voice was right next to her. She gasped. Her heart pounded in her chest, but she didn't see the man in the darkness of the parking lot. The yellowish shine of the two streetlights farther up the road didn't reach far enough.

If Melissa had been able to see more clearly in the darkness, she might have made out the shadow of a man with glittering black eyes and the traces of bloody fingerprints on his cheek. But it was a night dark as coal, and no moon showed behind the rain clouds over the town. Nobody saw the figure of Mr. Hutchinson. An old, weathered door opened with a shrieking sound in the adobe wall.

Not a single soul in town heard Melissa scream as he dragged her through that small entrance. Nobody witnessed her disappearance, and no one observed how the door vanished after it closed behind the Bird Cage pimp.

Melissa never returned home after that rainy, cold night, but no one missed the woman. She didn't have any family or a steady boyfriend. The man doing tequila shots with her certainly wasn't going to look for her again. She was known as a tramp, and nobody cared for her.

In the middle of the night the famous Bird Cage Theatre lives on, maintaining its reputation as the wildest honky-tonk throughout the frontier. The three huge front windows stare out onto Allen Street. The museum offers a great variety of artifacts of Tombstone's heydays, but more than that, it is one of the most haunted buildings in the entire U.S. Beware of the Gateway as it works only in one direction for those who are still alive and who dare to mingle with the spirits of those who never left town.

AUTHOR'S NOTE

I dedicate this book to the soiled doves of Tombstone's red-light district and to the outstanding Bird Cage Theatre, one of the most iconic frontier saloons and brothels that ever existed. The shady ladies and their customers, including the hard-working miners, played an important role during the heydays of Tombstone.

Without either group of daring pioneers, Tombstone would never have grown into a big silver boom town and would have never lured the Earp Brothers or Doc Holliday, to say nothing of the many other famous characters, into the settlement.

There were only very limited choices for women to earn a living after becoming a widow or being divorced in the old days. Sometimes they simply got thrown out of their house, or their husband "lost" his wife over a game of poker.

Laundry maid was one job possibility but barely paid enough to make a living. It was extremely hard physical work. Most times the only other choice was prostitution. Women were often forced into the world's oldest trade, but there were also "calico queens" that chose the profession because of the high- income potential. Women were outnumbered in the frontier, and the men knew their worth. Sometimes the ratio was fifty men to one woman.

However, the chances were quite high of catching a disease, such as syphilis, or getting killed by a brutal lover.

Tombstone's town council earned a fortune from the shady ladies as each one had to pay a license fee in order to receive permission to perform her arts. One could say the soiled doves of Tombstone built up the town more than any cowboy or gunfighter did.

Many of the brothels were run by so-called madams who took fifty percent of the customer's fee. But often enough, brothels were also turned into hospitals when some sort of disease raged through a town. The "pure" women looked down on the women of ill repute. Strangely, their donated money earned in sin was accepted and appreciated, nevertheless. For example, a large percentage of the contributions toward the building fund for The Church of Tombstone was money paid by the working girls of Sixth Street. Society had its share of hypocrites just like nowadays.

Tombstone hosted over one hundred ten saloons and fourteen gambling halls. It is said that over twelve hundred prostitutes "performed" their trade in the town during the mining heyday, most likely even more. The exact number has not been confirmed, but records of hundreds of city licenses issued for prostitution provide an estimate.

The most astonishing fact may be that a license with the name of Josephine Marcus, issued by Wyatt Earp, was found. It could be a forgery, but the lady was later better known under her husband's name, Josephine Marcus Earp. She tried to hide her shady past in Tombstone for the rest of her life. Since Wyatt was involved with the law in Tombstone, it wouldn't astonish folks if he really issued such a trade license.

The price of the girls' services per sexual favor varied from fifty cents to over twenty dollars or even more in pure silver or in gold coins, which was outrageous those days. Race, beauty, and youth, but also education and cleverness, dictated the price a man had to pay. Some fallen angels were comparable to nowadays movie stars and equally famous.

The shady ladies mentioned in this book were real performers of their trade at the famous Bird Cage Theatre.

Mae Davenport

Mae came into town with a circus group like many other women of her kind. She decided to stay in Tombstone and performed at the Bird Cage as a soiled dove and entertainer. Only one picture of her was published, showing her in the 1880s version of striped hot pants and lace-up ballet shoes. She was a slim, pretty woman with dark curly hair. Her prostitution license can be seen in the Bird Cage Museum along with her picture.

She saved her money and later started her own bordello in the Mexican town of Cananea. Many Tombstone working girls joined her there, in Mae's employ. This indicates that Mae was very likely respected among the girls or they wouldn't have joined her house of ill repute.

Lizette "The Flying Nymph"

Lizette's last name and her origin are unknown. She earned her nickname from the act she performed at the Bird Cage Theatre, appearing to "oat across the stage and above the audience on extremely thin, nearly invisible steel wires attached to a belt under her costume. She made her trapeze act alluring to attract more customers into her bed. Originally, she came to Tombstone with the Monarch Carnival Company and, like so many, chose to remain as a soiled dove.

Lizette soon developed depression and became an alcoholic. She was said to be unstable with extreme mood swings and self-destructive tendencies. Nowadays she would be diagnosed with bipolar personality. It is said that she committed suicide by taking an opium overdose. Lizette was an exceptional beauty with long, curly hair the color of copper. Her face was delicate like her petite figure. Pictures of her exist in different books.

Crazy Anne

The character was inspired by Dutch Annie, who was indeed a fallen angel of Tombstone's red-light district but not only that. She was a successful madam running one of the houses of ill fame. She was the secret queen of the red-light district and friends with everyone. Dutch Annie was known as a smart, friendly, and beautiful woman. When the outstanding, well-loved madam died, most of the population of Tombstone followed her coffin to Boot Hill where she is buried. Her real name remains a mystery, but her nickname suggests that she might have been of German heritage. A picture of her can be seen in Ben E. Traywick's books *Hell's Belles* and *Behind the Red Lights.*

William Tattenbaum aka Russian Bill

Russian Bill came to Arizona during the mid-1870s. He had long, dark-blond hair and kept an immaculate mustache, which added to his handsome looks. He also wore expensive clothing. He was quite well-liked among the females at the Bird Cage Theatre. William claimed to be the son of a wealthy Russian countess of German heritage and told people that he had served in the czar's army but had to free from there for attacking his superior officer. Due to his story, he earned the nickname Russian Bill, but his true name was William Tattenbaum, which is indeed a German name. What speaks for his tale of being of noble heritage is the fact that he was well-educated and spoke four languages fluently. The Russian nobleman was able to carry on fine conversations about science, literature, or the arts, to name but a few topics. History has it that he was friends with Curly Bill, Johnny Ringo, and Ike Clanton during his time in Tombstone. He wanted to be an outlaw like them and joined in some cattle rustling action but was not taken seriously. Unlike in the book, he eventually left Tombstone when the confrontation between the Earps and the Clantons seemed unavoidable. He teamed up with an outlaw named Sandy King whom he met in the mining town. They moved to Shakespeare, New Mexico. One day King, who was known as a bully and troublemaker, shot a storekeeper, injuring him severely. Russian Bill was not in town that day. However, an angry mob seized both when he returned to Shakespeare and hanged them without a fair trial. According to reports, Russian Bill begged for his life, but nobody in town showed any mercy. King is said to have only begged for a glass of water, claiming his throat was dry and sore from talking so much in order to save his life. The bodies were left hanging for days as a warning for other outlaws that the town of Shakespeare did not accept rowdy behavior.

When the people of Tombstone heard about Russian Bill's demise, they were sorry to have lost the man whose manners and company they had enjoyed as much as his riches, although they never believed his story. Strangely, legend has it that two years later a gentleman appeared in Tombstone representing a Russian Countess named Telfrin, the name Russian Bill had often mentioned as his mother's whenever he spoke of his roots. The stranger sought William Tattenbaum on behalf of Countess Telfrin who was searching for her long-lost son.

Word was soon sent back to Russia that the man had died of consumption because no one dared to tell the detective the truth about Russian Bill having been lynched over a minor crime by the locals in Shakespeare, New Mexico.

As for Russian Bill being a regular guest inside the famous Bird Cage Theatre, the museum claims that he rented his own poker booth for many months on a daily basis and had paid an outrageous amount in pure silver coins to the owner, whose name was indeed Hutchinson. William Tattenbaum's booth and gambling table can still be seen to the left of the big stage at the Bird Cage Museum.

Curly Bill Brocius

Not only was William "Curly Bill" Brocius a member of the gang of cowboys and a cattle rustler but also a tax collector for Sheriff Johnny Behan in Tombstone. He had a mean temper, especially when drunk, and often used gunfire to get people to obey his crazy ideas. One day he made a priest "dance" by firing at his feet with his six shooter while the clergyman was giving a sermon. Needless to say, how terrified the man of the good book must have been.

On October 28, 1880, Brocius shot the well-liked marshal, Fred White, in Tombstone. He was high on opium and claimed that his gun discharged accidently and feared he would be lynched. The severely wounded White himself testified that he thought it was an accident and that Brocius had not shot him on purpose. Curly Bill was exonerated. Sadly, Marshal White died two days later. Unlike the Hollywood movie versions, there is no proof that Curly Bill was involved in the assassination of Morgan Earp. However, Wyatt Earp and his associates were convinced of his guilt. Wyatt Earp ran into Curly Bill at Iron Springs on March 24, 1882. Earp shot Brocius with buckshot to the stomach, almost cutting Curly Bill in half.

Nellie Cashman

Nellie was a pretty Irish girl who arrived in Tombstone shortly after the Earp brothers in 1880. She started a restaurant and boarding house called The Russ House and sold meals for fifty cents. The building still stands nowadays and hosts the "Russ House bed and breakfast" now. Nellie always raised money for charity and the needy. Being a devout Catholic, she talked the owners of a well-known saloon—including Wyatt Earp—into permitting services there every Sunday until the church was built. But not only that. She also helped sick miners to receive medical treatment whenever needed and carried the well-deserved nickname "angel of the camp." Later on, she followed the gold rush to the Northern territories and raised the five children of her sister who had died of consumption way too young. Nellie Cashman died in 1925 in British Columbia.

The Bird Cage Theatre

The famous entertainment building was indeed widely known throughout the West and even in some Eastern cities. When Hutchinson and his wife opened its doors on December 26, 1881, it started as a twenty-four hour, seven-day a week establishment that soon turned into a legend.

It is a fact that the soiled doves used it as their favorite playground. Not only drinks were served but also other pleasures offered to the gents in thirteen small "cribs" overlooking the stage area. These gave the theatre its name as the girls reminded the men of little birds due to the feathers on their costumes and the cribs as bird cages since they were built right under the ceiling high above the floor. The famous song "A Bird in a Gilded Cage" is based on the Bird Cage Theatre's history. Those cribs and two larger bordello chambers in the basement speak a clear language of the building's sinful past.

The longest poker game of frontier times was held in the very basement of the Bird Cage. Legend says it lasted more than eight years, five months, and three days and was never interrupted. The story goes that the wood floor could not be completed under the table as nobody wanted to interrupt the game for carpentry work. Approximately one hundred forty bullet holes and documentation of twenty-six people being killed in the theatre during its heyday give an impression of how rough the past of the mining boomtown had been. Unlike many of the original structures along Allen Street, the Bird Cage Theatre with its adobe walls never burned down during the two big fires that raged through Tombstone destroying entire blocks. The theatre and brothel closed in 1889 when the major mining corporations gave up on their mines due to groundwater floodings. The history of the building itself is amazing. Nowadays, the Bird Cage is one of the most astonishing museums found in the Southwest and owned by the Hunley family in its fourth generation. Many items on display include weapons, clothes, household items, instruments, gambling equipment, and more. Visitors can experience an insight into daily life and the hardships during Tombstone's rowdy past. These days the Bird Cage offers paranormal tours as well and for good reason. Many have witnessed paranormal activities and were able to take pictures of it, especially around the funeral hearse. Famous ghost-hunting TV productions have shot series of investigations at the theatre and occasionally people witness orbs, weird lights, piano music, traces of perfumes and women laughing, transparent shadows, and much more. Even during the late '50s, citizens of Tombstone avoided walking by the closed building due to the weird sounds they witnessed coming from inside the theatre. The Bird Cage remains one of the most inspiring places to explore for me as a Western writer, and even after countless visits I never grow tired of walking through it. It is a must see for me during each Tombstone trip and offers a window into the pioneer past.

The Black Moriah

The funeral hearse known as the "Black Moriah" had been the last ride for most of the people that had passed during the silver boom in town, according to local records. Its value as an artifact, as well as for the gold and silver trim, runs around two million dollars nowadays, according to the insurance of the Bird Cage owner's family. The Black Moriah is the last of its kind built by James Cunningham and sons in Rochester and was sold to the undertaker Watt & Tarbell in Tombstone for eight thousand dollars. Tom and Frank McLaury, who got shot by the Earp brothers in the famous O.K. Corral gunfight, were transported to Boot Hill in this very hearse.

ABOUT THE AUTHOR

As someone born and raised in Germany, author Manuela Schneider's love of Native American and Western history might be surprising to some. But her fascination with pioneer life, cowboy heroes, and treacherous outlaws have been her constant companion for as long as she can remember.

Schneider recalls American TV shows like *Gun Smoke, Little House on the Prairie,* and *Bonanza* mesmerized her as a child.

In her adult years, Schneider fueled her deep interest in the American West by traveling to the U.S. and visiting historic sites like Tombstone, Monument Valley, and Kanab, Utah.

Experiencing the wild beauty of the Southwest firsthand made her desire to write stories of love, struggle, and survival in the wild, wild West even stronger.

After leaving a successful career in designing motorcycle fashion for the European market, Schneider penned her first Western novel in 2017. To date, Schneider has written seven books that often feature strong female characters who are immersed in a battle against hardship, riddles, and deception while searching for true love and a better life. Drawing energy from powerful pioneer women of our past, this vibrant author endeavors to create captivating sagas that ultimately leave readers wondering, *Will the story continue?*

Three new books are in the publishing process at present. Another four manuscripts are expected to be written by early 2024. Each published book has won awards at different festivals.

Her co-written song, "Miner's Candle," and its accompanying video has achieved great recognition and multiple awards in Arizona, Texas, California, New Mexico, and Europe. The song is played in seven countries worldwide.

When not researching or penning riveting stories about Western boomtowns and Native Americans, Schneider can be found traveling all over the world or studying at writing workshops. She also writes a Western travel blog on her website, http://www.manuelaschneider.com